PLEX PRESENTS

NO TURNING...

A BIG NATION EPIDEMIC
BADLAND PUBLISHING
www.badlandpub.com

I0684866

Cover Design Created by: Cedric "Ckillz" Killings & PLEX
Cover Graphics by: Cedric "Ckillz" Killings
Book Design by: Pam Quigley
Typed by: Michael Brown
Edited by: PLEX

This book is a work of fiction. Names, characters, places, and incidents are product of the author's imagination, or are used ficticiously. Any resemblance to actual events or locales or persons living, or dead, is entirely coincidental.

NO TURNING...
A BIG NATION EPIDEMIC
Published By:
BADLAND PUBLISHING/PLEX PRESENTS
P.O. Box 11623
Riviera Beach, Fl. 33419
ISBN: 978-0-9825018-8-7

(C) Copyright 2011 Nathan Welch

For more information log on to www.badlandpub.com

Ain't Nobody Pen'in Like Us, Man !!!

DEDICATION

FOR LATASHA AND LUNDON

FROM REGGO

ACKNOWLEDGEMENTS

First, All praises are due to ALLAH; The creator of all the Worlds, and everything that exist. Thank you for blessing me with the talent and patience to paint a picture on paper!
To my man PLEX thanks for showing the love where it counts. I hope to continue what we started on this joint right here. Now let's get this money ! Things happen for a reason slim, you know what I mean about the delay.

To Tiah Short, thanks for giving me the first shot to introduce my work to the world. Without you, I never would've got the chance to express my wild imagination and dreams on paper. DC Book Diva will shine, especially when your debut book drops.

To Eyone Williams, and Aisha Bailey, thanks for being the first ones to take notice of my talent. When one door closes another one always open up. I appreciate everything ya'll did for me during this struggle. I wish ya'll all the best in your endeavors. Eyone, you did your thing on "Hell Razor Honeys" too...

To all the fans and readers of the urban genre, this is my second joint in print, and I could've never done it without ya'll... Your thirst for new stories give me the reason to strive harder to out do all the competition. I hope you enjoy.

To my mother, thanks for being mean to me. This is for you OLe' Lady, maybe this will help you get the big house that you've always wanted. I Love You!

To My family Mortisha P. Grey, Henry Welch, and Sidney Pegram Jr. Thanks for everything that ya'll have done and not done for me during this time in the struggle. Hopefully I can return the favor after I reach the Best Sellers list.

To All my homies and good men I met during my incarceration, I hope you buy a copy of this joint and support the hustle. You know how it is. It's too many of ya'll to name, so If you remember me then sign your name here _____ for my shout out to you. It's nothing but Love Homeboy!!!

Last but not least to my Get Familiar Family: Talk Sick, MILK, and CLINTON SPARKS, thanks for putting me down with IntalkSicating INK. I'll try to give you only the hot shit, and not the Hot Garbage....

Finally to all haters. Keep doing what you do, so I can keep laughing and brushing my shoulders off with you lames.

OFF DA' RULER'S DESK

...it's funny how one man's success can be another man's pain. And seeing just how successful we are over here at BADLAND PUBLISHING/PLEX PRESENTS; I know that there are beaucoup people suffering. For that we will not apologize. Our plan is to turn up the heat with every release. However, we do understand that this great success which we are experiencing would not be possible without YOU the reader...Our aim is to deliver one best-seller at a time. We offer our people (the readers) affordable entertainment that can be reread or passed on to others at anytime, because our classic tales are never out dated!!! Through your support we are able to give back to our communities through legal relief funds and programs for troubled youth... Though our books express the grim realities of inner-city life, we in no way intend to promote violence or the mis-education of our people. Our authors only mean to entertain, express the ills of bad decisions, and better their current situations... Everyday we're losing more and more black lives to disease and senseless black-on-black violence. Because of that there's been an onslaught of racially bias laws inacted to further destroy (us) as a people... It's a sad day when a mother (a family) loses her son or daughter to a wickedly unjust system. Yet it's far more devastating when a mother loses her son or daughter to senseless violence... Part of our responsiblity at BADLAND PUBLISHING/PLEX PRESENTS/BOOK-GANG MEDIA is to provide a platform for the voiceless, so I'd like to share a few words of sentiment from a real sweet and loving mother whom recently lost her (only) son to the ignorance of the streets...[She wrote] *my mind is gone and my heart is so broken without Darryl. I feel so alone. Not a day goes by that my eyes don't fill up with tears. I miss him so much! My life seems to be over without him. I don't know where to start to get my life back together. I worked so hard to become a nurse, but I barely work now because it really doesn't mean a whole lot without my baby here to see me come-up. They don't know what they took from me. They could have just killed me, because I'm the one who's life is (now) over...* I'm asking that you all please consider Bridgette's woeful words before acting out without fully realizing the ramifications of your thoughtless actions... I got Gorilla Convict/Shortside tattooed under my left eye and BOOK GANG/ BADLAND under my right, because that's all I see! The future is ours, so GET DOWN or LAY DOWN...

ONE LOVE,
PLEX

Chapter 1
MA-Duke's Ultimatum

"BOY! I'LL BEAT YOUR MOTHERFUCKIN' ASS! I DON'T KNOW WHO THE FUCK YOU THINK YOU'RE TALKIN TO MISTER! I BROUGHT YOU INTO THIS WORLD! AND I'LL TAKE YOU OUT! NOW POP SLICK OUT THE MOUTH AGAIN, HEAR!" His moms, Patricia Weaver, shouted at him after she heard him mumble under his breath, "I can't stand your ass."

Technically Ramel was wrong for disrespecting his Ma-Dukes, but sometimes he just had to respond. Ms. Weaver was overprotective, strict, and had the most nagginess ways one would ever see in a woman. If you saw Ms. Weaver, on the street, you would never assume that the 5'4", sepia-toned, petite, nice-looking woman was a fucking ALTER BEAST to her last baby boy. Her oldest son, Rico, got killed in 1998, and her second oldest, Randy, was serving a life sentence in prison for avenging his brother's death. So, one would guess that she was just trying to hold on to her son and stop the inevitable, little Ramel from leaving the nest at age 14 to play in the wicked streets!

"RAMEL! BOY, DON'T MAKE ME COME IN THERE AND FUCK YOU UP! NOW ANSWER ME! WHO THE FUCK ARE YOU TALKING TO?" she yelled from the living room of their two-bedroom apartment, invading his thoughts. Before Ramel could answer, she burst into his room, and gave him an evil look, which Ramel hated.

Ms. Weaver was furious and cursing like a drunk sailor. She had a quick temper, especially as of lately. It was behind all of the broads that had been calling and asking for her son at all times of the day and night.

To be honest, Ramel didn't see why she was mad. He could see if he was a girl and a bunch of guys were blowing the spot up, or a bunch of gay guys were calling her son, then it'd be time to be furious! Ramel, in his young mind, thought that by giving out his numbers to all of the lovely women that he met on a daily basis, his moms would be proud and know that she didn't raise no fags -- boy, was he wrong!

"ANOTHER LIL' SLUT CALL MY HOUSE AT 2:30 IN THE DAMN MORNING, ASKING FOR YOUR ASS RAMEL!" She shouted, startling him.

"YOU THINK IT'S CUTE TO BE OUT THERE FUCKING ALL THEM GIRLS RAMEL? YOU STICKING YOUR DICK IN THEM GIRLS, AND I BET THAT YOU'RE NOT USING ANY CONDOMS, NOR KNOW IF ANY OF THEM GIRLS ARE CLEAN FORM A.I.D.S, AND ALL THE OTHER SHIT THAT YOU CAN CATCH NOWADAYS?" She shouted and knocked over the X-Box 360 video game that sat on the bureau, her eyes blazing with anger.

"Ma, stop tripping. I'm not doing anything," he lied quickly, trying to mask the fear that engulfed him.

Ms. Weaver was a woman that didn't mind getting in her son's face. Even though she had to look up at his 6'2", brown paper bag colored frame. Truth be told, he still felt like a little boy, so he quickly looked away.

"Look at you! You dress like one of them fucking thugs outside, and them rappers that you watch on B.E.T. What the hell is wrong with you? Have you learned anything from your brothers' mistakes?" She asked, glaring at him, disapproving of the route her son was taking in life. Ramel, young and dumb, figured that she was at the point where she would either keep nagging him to get him on the right path, whatever that was, or just let him go so that he could do him!

He didn't have time to hear that shit. It was a scorching mid-June day in the city where it goes down, and Ramel wanted to leave so he could sport his gear. Fresh in some black H.O.B.O. baggy cargo shorts, a white tight tank-top, some white slouch socks, and a fresh pair of tan Timberlands. He had his hair tight, laid back with nine french braids—courtesy of a cutie that he'd fucked real good the other night. Ramel didn't look like the average 14 year old. He had a well developed mustache and beard

2

in which he kept at a shadow's length. His big brother, Randy, stayed on top of him from the pen' about working out; so he had developed cuts and muscles in all the right places. As the product of a Dominican father and Mulatto mother, his mixed heritage got him the attention of many young girls in the hood and older broads around the city.

"BOY, IF YOU DON'T ANSWER ME!" She shouted, sticking her tiny finger in his face, poking him in the forehead extremely hard.

Ms. Weaver hated the road that her youngest son was trying to take, dressing like some thug on the street corner. She knew her son was a handsome and intelligent young man, but he was moving too wreckless. She dreaded seeing her baby boy end up like her other two sons and his father had -- victims of the wicked streets. She wanted her son to have something better than that wasted life.

Even though she tried her hardest to turn him away, Ms. Weaver saw in her son what she saw in his father when they'd first met. They were attracted to the FAST LANE. Which consisted of FAST MONEY, FAST CARS, FAST WOMEN, AND A FASTER DEATH DATE!

Ms. Weaver knew that her son was enthralled by all of the gangster stories he'd heard about his drug dealing father and thugged-out brothers. She also believed that he was already in that lifestyle, she just couldn't catch him! Yet it was slowly coming out. She figured that no decent young woman would call a young man's house that late sounding all sexy, just to talk. It was a BOOTY CALL! She had angrily picked up the telephone that had disturbed her sleep and heard the young woman say, "Ramel, can you come scratch your Kitty-Kat?"

"NO HE CANNOT, YOU LIL' HOE." Ms. Weaver went off . "Bitch, my son is fourteen years old! Fourteen! Don't ever call here for him again, you cradle-robbing-pressed-for-some-dick-gold-digging ass bitch!" She ended her verbal tirade by slamming down the telephone. She then tossed and turned the rest of the night, itching to confront her son about the late night phone calls and the other things that he was doing that rubbed her the wrong way.

3

"Yeah, I've learned from them." Ramel finally answered, trying to get the verbal abuse over with so that he could go chick-hunting.

"You couldn't have, because you're doing the same shit!" She fired back. "Keep it up, here! I swear if I catch you fucking in my house, or find out that you got one of these fast ass girls around here pregnant, I'ma fuck you up! Then I'ma put your ass out! So go ahead and be like your damn father and brothers, Ramel. But remember this, the first time your ass get into some shit out there in them streets, don't come running to me for help. They sure do have a place for your ass. Just ask your know-it-all-brother the next time that he calls here begging for some money. Matter of fact, just go to the fucking cemetary where your daddy and brother are rotting with bullet holes in their damn skulls!"

That did it for him! Ramel couldn't hold his anger in any longer. *Why she had to go there about my pops and Rico? They only been gone for two years, but it still hurts like it was yesterday. I gotta check her about that shit! Whatever happens just happens!* He thought, never knowing that he was speeding up the wheels of his destiny.

"You're fucked up for real, Ma! Why you always gotta talk bad about Pops and Rico like that? You always talking shit abou---"

He was quickly silenced by a hard slap across his left cheek. If she hadn't given him birth, Ramel would've went Bernard Hopkins on her and beat her ass to a no count.

"DON'T YOU EVER COME OUT THE SIDE OF YOUR FACE AT ME LIKE THAT AGAIN! I AM YOUR MOTHER, YOU DUMB MOTHERFUCKER! I'M TRYING TO SHOW YOUR STUPID ASS WHERE YOU'RE GONNA END UP IF YOU KEEP DOING THE SHIT THAT YOU'RE DOING!"

"I'M NOT DOING SHIT, MA!" he shouted, pushing her on the bed. He could hear, "RAMEL, C'MERE! RAMEL, GET YOUR ASS BACK IN HERE OR ELSE! RAMEL, IF YOU DON'T BRING YOUR ASS BACK IN HERE RIGHT NOW, THEN DON'T EVER COME BACK AGAIN! YOU HEAR ME?"

Ramel stopped with the quickness after hearing her ultimatum.

4

Was he ready to take on the world alone? How would he survive in a city where all the weak muthafuckas died? He was damned if he didn't and damned if he did? *So watch a young muthafucka pull a vicious move*, he told himself and took off running without looking back, totally ignoring his crazy mother's deafening screams....

Chapter 2
My Dawg's Father

Once Ramel reached the dark stairwell, he slowed down enough to wipe away some more tears from his face. Walking down the pissy smelling stairwell he noticed two figures sitting at the bottom stairs with their backs turned to him.

They stared cautiously at one another as the man and woman sat close together, flicking a lighter. Ramel automatically knew that they were crackheads. No person in their right frame of mind would be hiding away from the hood in the bowels of some funky project steps unless they were tricking with a crackhead, selling dope to a crackhead, or smoking the poison that created crackheads.

When he got up on them, they both turned quickly and looked up at him. The man's hair was nappy, clothes in disarray, and the woman was gripping a long crack pipe in her hand, trying to get the lighter to work. Their eyes looked drowsy, as if they hadn't slept in days.

"Ra..." The man smiled, revealing yellow stained crooked teeth. "Ramel, what's up youngster?" He asked, eyeing his get high partner suspiciously, as if she were trying to get over on him.

"Ain't shit, Lonzo." Ramel muttered, feeling ashamed and disappointed to see him like that. It was really fucked up and just a reminder of what could happen to the weak ones in these evil streets. It was also motivation for him, because he was determined to win and not let the hood take him under.

He'd never seen Alonzo "Lonzo" Davis like that before. Alonzo was four years older than himself, he had attended high school and hustled with Ramel's brother, Rico. They had both been the most popular, best-dressed, and straight up dudes one could ever meet in the hood. They had been voted the "Most Likely To

Win The Game" by the streets. Now, his brother was taking a dirt nap and Alonzo was out there smoking on the same poison that he once got paid off. From the looks of things, Lonzo was probably broke and homeless. He'd heard that Alonzo had been so stressed out after Rico's demise that he'd smoked some crack to escape the pain and ended up getting hooked on it.

"You tryna flow pass, youngster?" Lonzo asked, looking impatient.

"Ain't nuffin' young about me no more Lonzo!" Ramel hissed, causing them to move against the wall, allowing him passage.

"My bad, soldier!" Lonzo said sarcastically, holding up his hands in mock surrender.

As Ramel passed them he looked Alonzo hard in the face and saw the damage that the poison had done. Alonzo turned away quickly, diverting his attention to the woman and then to the crack pipe.

The woman was Anita-Boo. She looked even worse than Alonzo. Back in the days, Nita-Boo was the most sought after dime piece in the hood, so Lonzo made her his bun-bun. She was loyal to him in every way, seeing as she was still with his ass and allowing herself to fall off in a major way, chasing that poison. She looked at Ramel and sucked her teeth loudly. That was his cue. Ramel didn't say a word. He left the building, and emerged into the cruddy streets of Southeast. The most notorious section of Washington, D.C.

Confused, Ramel wanted to escape his mother's wrath at all cost. He didn't want to return home, but he was fourteen with no where to lay his head. He missed his pops and brothers dearly, but also knew that it was a 95% chance that he'd end up like them if he didn't play the streets cautiously, with a cold heart and military mind. Alonzo, his Pops, Rico, and Randy were examples of costly mistakes that he could never commit! Ramel wasn't going to let the streets fuck him over -- not even at gunpoint!

Trekking down the street to his partner Flat's apartment, Ramel contemplated his next move, persuasion. He needed to get Flat to let him stay at his spot until he came up with other living arrangements.

7

Reginald "Flat-Head" Belle was two years older than Ramel and had known him since he was six. They went to the same schools and had similar taste in broads. The two both loved messing with the young gold-diggers in training, who flaunted their bodies and promised them everything in hopes of getting their young riches. Of course, neither was rich, yet what one had, so did the other.

Ramel knocked hard on Flat's door. Then appeared his stocky father, yanking open the door.

"Boy, is you outta' your damn mind?" Mr. Belle said, voice dripping with venom. He greeted Ramel with a fucked up look.

Mr. Sidney Belle was a 6'6" big black, stocky man in his mid-forties. He had prison tattoos, a shiny bald head and a face that only his mother could love. Mr. Belle was jive cool. Probably because he'd been to prison and was now doing social work to prevent youngsters from entering America's penal systems.

"No Sir. I jus--"

"Just shit!" He cut Ramel off. " Look boy, your mother just called here looking for you. She told me to call her if you showed up. Now tell me what's up, before I have to tackle your ass and take you home." He said, opening the door and giving Ramel that mean-ass parental look as he walked into the apartment.

"It's like this Mr. B," Ramel sighed. "My mufa' keeps kirking out on me for no reason so I left, plain and simple."

"Plain and simple, huh?" He asked, scratching his long beard. " So where are you going to go?"

Ramel just shrugged his shoulders in reply to the million dollar question. He couldn't even think straight. The only thing that was on his mind was *WHERE AM I GOING TO GO?*

"Peep game, Ramel. Do you think for one second that if your mother didn't love you, that she'd stay on yo' case like she does? "

"You love Fla--, I mean Reggo', and you never press him out like my mufa' does me. I'm tired of that shit, slim. Excuse my language, sir."

"Ramel, it's a different scenario. I understand what's going on out there, and I have to be there for my son in ways that no man has ever been there for me. So I let Reggo' learn things the hard

8

way and school him as he grows. Oh, best believe if he gets too big headed, I'ma drop this big right hand on his flat head ass." He smirked, holding up a massive fist, revealing the fact that he knew about Reggo's nickname.

Mr. Belle held Ramel captive for another twenty-minutes, giving him a lecture on the do's and don't's of how to succeed in society without doing the things that would get him a life sentence behind bars. Even though he was spitting some deep science, young Ramel only stored some of it in the brain. The rest went in one ear and straight out the other!

"So keep that in mind Ramel, you hear?" He said, disturbing Ramel's thoughts. "And I'll tell your mother that I haven't seen you, okay."

"Good looking, Mr. B!" he exclaimed with a sigh of relief. Ramel just knew that he would send his ass back home after the lecture.

"I'ma talk to your mother and see if I can work something out where you can come stay with us during the week and stay with her on the weekends for the summer, until ya'll stop beefing."

"For real?" he gasped. "Slim, I mean, Mr. B, if you can do that for me, that would be the sweetest."

"I'ma try. If I pull it off you owe me one, Ramel."

"You got that, champ!" Ramel giggled. "Is Flat up in here?"

"Yeah, he's in his room." Mr. Belle said.

Ramel got up and walked down the hallway to Flat's bedroom with the weight of the world lifted off of his young shoulders.

But for how long?

Chapter 3
The Metamorphosis

Once Ramel entered Flat's bedroom, he saw him pacing back and forth in nothing but his boxers. Ramel was somewhat jealous of his tight six pack, because Flat didn't work out at all; while he'd been putting in major work, diligently sculpting his body. Yet his shit was not even close to Flat's shit.

"C'mon slim, put some clothes on," he blurted out and flopped down on Flat's huge waterbed.

"Ramel, why the fuck is you at my joint so mothafuckin' early? Your geekin' ass know I don't hit the block until after twelve." Flat grumbled as the waves of the bed began to settle.

Flat-Head was about 5'9", medium build, with burnt copper skin and light-brown eyes. His dome was mushed in freakishly in the rear, thus creating his well known alias "Flat-Head".

"Slim, I had to get ghost. Ma-Dukes lunching again. She talking all crazy and shit about Pops and my brothers. Man, fuck that shit." Ramel sucked his teeth angrily.

"What my baby-mufa' beefin' for this time?" He smirked, trying to make Ramel mad. *It worked!*

"Flat, don't get fucked up in your own joint!"

"What!" Was all Flat said. He then darted into his closet and quickly returned holding a chunky chrome semi-automatic handgun.

"You ain't ready for me, Ramel." Flat smiled devishly and cocked the weapon. "I don't do no more fighting. I'm giving out dirt naps with the quickness though. You want one?"

He better be playing. He my man, I know he'd never think about bringing me any harm? Or would he? Ramel thought.

"A'ight, keep on playing with me, slim." he finally barked.

"I don't give a fuck about you kirking out!" Flat said and

10

aimed the gun at Ramel's legs. "I know you pump faking! Straight up!" He teasingly said while waving the pistol around to drive his point home.

Flat-Head had a way he talked to people. It was in an aggressive tone and he'd always use his hands, just like his father. He did that in an effort to size up his man for a sneak attack, knockout punch; just in case he didn't like the person's feedback. Flat-Head was wild like that.

"STOP PLAYING FLAT, DAMN!" Ramel yelled and jumped, causing Flat to jump back and erupt with laughter.

"AAHH!" He laughed his ass off. "You was scared as shit. You was sweating worser than a pimp with one hoe!"

"Yeah, whatever." Ramel said, trying to hold in his laughter.

Even on his gloomiest day, his man Flat-Head always found a way to make him feel good.

"On some get serious shit, what's your mufa' lunching about?" He asked and gave Ramel the gun.

When he held it he couldn't believe something that small was powerful enough to take a human life. At that moment he began wondering what it would feel like to kill someone. Did he even have the balls to do it?

"Earth to geekin' moe!" Flat said, saucily, invading his thoughts.

"Oh, Moms lunching because this lil' bitch called for me off the late night. I don't know what she said, but Moms is under the impression that I'm fucking her."

"Nigga, you is." Flat-Head chuckled as Ramel gave him back the pistol. He knew that if he held it any longer he'd grow attached to it, which was something he didn't need right then.

"Yeah, but she don't need to know my business. All she does is throw the shit up in my face, and keep saying I'ma end up just like my Pops and brothers."

"That's fucked up slim, straight up! I miss the shit outta Rico and Randy." He confessed, which was rare. Flat-Head always played the *I don't give a fuck about nobody role*; so Ramel really began believing that he was a heartless individual.

"Life goes on, champ." Ramel said quickly, trying to deter

Flat from going down memory lane, and opening up old wounds.

They were the only two up and coming young niggas out on the block during his brother's reign around Linda-Pollin projects. By the time other kids reached the age of 10 and 12, and began playing little league sports, Flat and Ramel were hanging with the big-boys; doing big boys things and being with all the people who were making that got-damn noise.

"No bullshit. That's why I gotta come up, straight up!" Flat said, laying a pair of prison grey Solbiato Sport sweatpants across the bed. Solbiato clothing apparel was like Versace and other high price fashion designs, but it was only made and popularized by the natives of D.C. Legend has it that the news of this exclusive gear reached all the way up to N.Y.C., bringing people to D.C. like Jay-Z, before the Hard Knock Life Tour, the late great Notorious B.I.G., Puff-Daddy and Lil' Kim. Basically what it boiled down to was if you sported that Solbiato shit, nine times out of ten you were getting a little cash.

"Me too, Flat. Fuck being broke and all fucked up for the summer. I just seen that weak ass joker Lonzo smoking crack with that has been, geekin' ass bitch, Nita-Boo. They looked bad too, slim."

"Stop playing, moe?" Flat blurted, as if he didn't believe what Ramel was saying.

"That's on my brother and Moe's grave. I can't see myself ever going out like that, Flat. That's for them weak ass jokers, for real. From now on I'm on *get money time,* all day everyday!"

"I feel you, scrap'." Flat said. "We dogs for life. You know what that means right?" He quizzed.

"Ride or Die to the fullest," Ramel added. "I got your back and front, and you better have mine, Flat."

"You know that goes without saying, straight up!" Flat said and began getting dressed.

Ramel laid on the bed and read the latest Urban Exposure Magazine.

After Flat-Head finished dressing in his fresh white tee, sweats and grey New Balance 1500 track shoes, they played a few games of '01 N.B.A. Live for $10 a game. They ended up breaking even. By that time it was close to 1 p.m., which meant it was time to hit the streets.

As they were leaving the apartment, Flat's father called Ramel. He figured it was to lay down his ground rules for his future stay.

"What's up, Mr. B?"

"Lemme' holler at you for a minute."

"Ay' slim, I'ma be out front." Flat gave him some dap and a one arm hug before leaving the apartment.

When Ramel walked into Mr. B's bedroom he noticed the strong stench of Marijuana, which was the drug he loved. He wanted to ask him could he smoke with him, but figured he could wait a few more minutes and smoke good with Flat-Head.

"Ramel," he sighed and shook his head in a sad way. Ramel knew that wasn't a good look.

"I was talking to your mother all morning. She even kirked out on me. I tried everything youngin', I just couldn't get her to bend. She batted me down about you coming to live with us for the summer. Plus she said she's calling the police and reporting you as a missing person. So you can't stay."

That's all Ramel heard, again feeling his young shoulders slump. The weight of the world had came crashing back down on him tenfold.

"What the fuck will I do?" he asked himself.

Mr. Belle droned on.

"Listen Ramel, it's not the end of the world. After you chill here tonight and get your mind right, just go home and face the music."

"To be honest Mr. B, I'm jive tired of that same old tune. I think it's time that I start creating my own music. They say that *God loves the child who has his own.*"

"That sounds good, killer." He retorted.

Ramel could hear the sarcasm dripping in his tone.

"What are you prepared to do to get your own? Just remember this; 'The prisons and cemetaries are triple bunking because of guys who had the same ambitions as you.' Them streets are real treacherous, and they don't give a fuck about you or me. Just be forever mindful about that. You are the architect of your destiny! Don't fuck it up by building yourself a prison cell or a goddamn pine box!"

"I won't, Mr. B, I won't." Ramel stated, meaning every word.

As he stood up and gave Ramel a supportive hug, Ramel imagined he was his Pops holding him and saying, "It's time to man up and take what you want in life, son!"

With that thought Ramel knew that he could never return home and subject himself to his Mom's emotional, physical, and verbal abuse. At that instant a metamorphosis happened; Ramel changed from a boy to a man.

Now realizing that it was him against the world. He knew what he had to do and that there definitely was NO TURNING BACK....

Chapter 4
Hot Pepa

It didn't take long for Ramel to find himself around Valley Avenue, inside the Infamous Valley Green Projects. The Valley and Linda Pollin Projects were seperated by a couple of main streets like Whaller Place and Southern Ave., but you could get to and fro both hoods within three minutes by walking.

Flat-Head had persuaded Ramel to go with him over some broad's house. It wasn't long before Flat was illustrating his hand movements as he talked to several dudes from The Valley.

Taking a break from the fucked up thoughts that Ramel was having about being homeless, he got high as a G-4 Lear jet with Flat and a few dudes from The Valley. This enhanced a marvelous collection of good thoughts, which in the beginning were always concerned with desperate measures to take care of himself.

While they chilled around The Valley, Ramel was struck by one female in particular. She was beautiful like an early collection of an Italian painting. She was a red-bone with smooth-unblemished skin and light-hazel eyes – like a cat depicting seductive beauty. She had to be about 5'3", 135 pounds, with curves in all the right places. Her ears showcased hoop earrings. Her Coco Chanel outfit showed that she had expensive taste and the stare that she kept throwing Ramel's way showed that she was interested in something about him.

"Ay' Flat, whose that bitch over there?" he asked, nodding in her direction. Flat and the guys turned to look.

"Oh, that's Pepa, slim." Mean-Gene spoke up.

Mean-Gene resembled a younger version of the Rapper/Hype-Man, Flavor Flav. He was similar to a lamp post in the hood; he was always around, stayed out of the way and shed light on them about everything that was happening in the hood. All in all, he was a good dude and an even better source of information. There's a Mean-Gene in every ghetto in America.

"Pepa who, nigga?" Flat stated aggressively as Ramel locked eyes with her. She quickly looked away and pretended to fumble around inside her Coach Bag.

Something about this female grabbed Ramel and held his interest, but he didn't know why? He stared at her for a long time, thinking about it. Then looking away, he found himself looking back at her. Interested, intrigued.

What made this female different from all the others in the hood? The answer came immediately! It wasn't just her. It was a collective of clothes, jewelry and apparent confident swagger, mounted together to sell herself as main-bun material. It was an advertisement.

It blew him away!

"I'm telling you Flat-Head, that bitch Pepa only fucks with them niggas that's getting that hank." Mean-Gene pointed out just as a butter-pecan colored Range Rover pulled up in front of Pepa.

"See what I'm saying." Mean-Gene added knowingly. He then nodded at the expensive vehicle.

The interaction between Pepa and the driver of the S.U.V. was the same as the visual relationship between a prostitute and a trick on the hoe stroll.

Ramel stared at Pepa for a long time, suddenly seeing two masked gunmen quickly run up on the Range Rover. Everything seemed to move in slow motion. It was a frightening and stunning moment.

The next thing that he heard was loud gunshots and horrific screams. Everyone dove for cover!

"NOT TODAY, BITCH NIGGAS! STRAIGHT UP!" he heard Flat-Head shouting.

Ramel looked up and saw Flat standing over one of the mask gunmen aiming the same gun at his head that he'd pulled earlier.

"WHAT THE FUCK IS YOU DOING!" Ramel

screamed. The driver of the Range Rover got out cocking a .357 Desert Eagle and kicked the gunman in the face.

The other gunman wasn't moving. A puddle of blood oozed from his head. Ramel assumed that he was somewhere trying to explain all of his past sins to God, in an effort to get up into Heaven.

Pepa screamed, looking on in horror, witnessing the brutal slaying. The dead gunman's blood flowed in the streets like the Anacostia River.

"OH MY GOD! OH MY GOD!" She yelled, then began backing towards her building, trying to reach safety.

"Shut the fuck up bitch!" Flat growled at her. The driver of the Range Rover pulled the mask off of the gunmen.

"You bitch-ass nigga! Your snake-ass s'pose to be my family!" Was all Ramel heard the driver bark before he began pistol whipping the downed man.

Ramel ran towards Pepa with a sense of urgency. He didn't know why he'd put his super-hero cape on, but he wanted to protect her from the evil that men do. Once he reached her, he tried to pull her inside of the building. Only to catch a swift gut-wrenching elbow for his bravery.

"GIRL, I'M TRYNA HELP YOUR RETARDED ASS!" he yelled.

"I DON'T NEED YOUR MUTHAFUCKIN' HEL--"

"BOOM! BOOM! BOOM!" guns continued calling.

The terrifying sounds of more gunshots ringing out ended all conversation. Sounds that Ramel dreaded. Sounds that had claimed the lives of his Pops and brother. Sounds that led him into Pepa's world.

All of a sudden, everything went still. Ramel looked up and saw Flat-Head jumping in the Range Rover with the driver. They calmly pulled off, leaving two bodies leaking in the streets. Ramel felt someone pulling on him. He turned and saw Pepa's face contorted in pain. Her pretty-hypnotic eyes filled with tears.

"Boy, you better c'mon before they come back shooting." Pepa cried out.

By now a crowd had began forming. So he ran behind

17

Pepa, and inside the building, fearing the worse for his partner Flat-Head.

What made him kill somebody in broad daylight? Had he killed before? Who was that dude driving the Range? And what does this broad have to do with all of this shit? He wondered as they reached her apartment.

When Pepa got to the door and saw Ramel behind her, she damn near dropped her keys from shaking so much.

"Calm down girl, yo--"

"CALM SHIT!" She yelled. "Two niggas just got killed in front of my face. Niggas don't leave no witnesses alive around here. I gotta get up out of here."

Hearing the fear in her tone, Ramel wrapped his arms around Pepa and looked at her with pleading eyes. Eyes that begged her to calm down. He guided her hand, holding the key into the lock and opened the door.

"They gonna kill me. I just know they are," she said sobbing. The apartment that they entered was nicely furnished.

They won't kill you if I can help it! he thought, watching her kick off her thigh high leather boots, revealing her small pretty feet. *Damn she's a beast,* his fourteen year old hormones screamed.

"No they won't." Ramel said and closed the door. All he had in the world was his word, a fistful of dollars, and a list full of problems. Hopefully Pepa won't add to that problem list.

"How do you know? You ain't God." Pepa shot back, invading his thoughts.

"You right, I'm not, but I'm willing to meet God to protect you from them jokers," he quickly blurted, not knowing where that lame ass shit just came from. He was tripping for real. It must have been his dick talking right then.

"For Real? You really mean that?" She asked in a baby's voice.

"Hell yeah," he lied quickly, seeing that that was his way in the door. His brother always told him the key to fucking a female physically, was to first fuck them mentally, so Ramel was going for what he knew. *What could it hurt?*

"And what do I have to give you in return? Some

18

pussy, I bet?" She questioned with her hands on her thick hips.

"Now, why you have to go there? Get your mind out of the gutter. I just like you shawdy, and I don't wanna see nothing happen to you, that's all." *Well not until I dick you down real good. Then you can go to hell for all I care,* Ramel thought with a smile on his face.

She revealed a Hollywood smile, alerting him that she was letting down her defenses. If she only knew what he was smiling for.

"I'm sorry…it's just been a wild day, ummm'..." she said, searching for his name.

"Ramel, they call me Ramel."

"I'm Pepa. I know this is a fucked up way to meet somebody, huh?"

"Not at all, Pepa. Everything happens for a reason." *Hopefully it's the reason that leads me between your thick legs,* he thought, watching her stand in the center of her living room, twirling one of her sandy-blond micro-extensions as if she was a little uncomfortable.

Putting aside his lust towards Pepa for a moment, Ramel walked up to her and held her for a long time, trying to ease all her fears.

"Do you feel like staying here with me for awhile?" She asked in a little girl tone. Shit reminded him of that singer Mich'elle.

"You got me for as long as you need, okay?"

She nodded and put her arms around him. As she led him to her bedroom, all he kept thinking was, *how can I work this bad broad to benefit me?*

Pepa led Ramel to her bed and they laid down, cuddling. All that day he held her in his arms; listening to her cry herself to sleep.

Once she was dead to the world he let his thoughts run wild. He began plotting on a way to seduce Pepa, so he would have a place to stay. At least until things got better for him....

Chapter 5
Watch For Snakes

"It's all about us, shawdy. I'ma make you a star, for real." The driver promised Flat-Head.

They were speeding along Indian Head Highway, thriving off of the adrenaline rush that come with commiting murder. The driver had just killed his first cousin, who tried to take him out of the GAME. It fucked him up to the point where he kept screaming his cousin's name, attaching *that bitch-ass-snake-ass nigga* on the end.

The driver was concentrating on the road and violating the speed limit while wiping sweat from his dark chocolate brow. His curly afro, which looked wet, made him look like a sexy R&B singer. The driver was known throughout the city as Fray, the big black drug dealer who resembled a younger version of the comedian Bernie Mack.

"My name's Flat, not shawdy. I got that name by putting in work like the shit you just saw. Straight up!" Flat-Head said after hearing the weak promises that the man gave. But he expected it.

Flat-Head knew that he would've said the same thing after a nigga had just saved his life. A nigga would be a damn fool not to promise his savior the world and everything in it.

"Oh yeah, so you be flat-lining shit, huh?" Fray asked.

"Straight up!" Flat-Head answered, looking straight ahead and watching the drug dealer in his peripheral vision. Flat-Head knew that it was wicked in the streets; and the only way to survive was to trust nobody but yourself and your guns! Anything else would be uncivilized!

"I like that shaw--, I mean, Flat. Watch Flat, it's gonna be you and me. I'm jive doing good for myself right now."

Who don't know that shit, Fray? That's why them niggas

just tried to bring you a move. It's a good thing I was in the right place at the right time. I just hope nobody starts snitching on me? That bitch Pepa was jive phat. I'd hate to have to kill her ass! So I hope she keeps her mouth shut... I wonder if I can fuck her now that she's seen my work? Flat contemplated, then asked Fray what his name was.

"It's Fray! Young nigga, you ain't hip to me?" Fray asked irritably, as if the youngster was suppose to know who he was.

Ferlando "Fray" Copeland was a slick talking hustler/killer who'd been under pressure his entire life. Fray grew up hard, but there he was, the caring relative, hoping for some sort of salvation for killing his cousin , who didn't give a damn about him. Fray was unprepared for that type of move, and it hurt. Rather than fight and reject the circumstances that landed him amid such despair, Fray did what seemed right. He was a young person who was raised by the code of the streets. So being logical, he relented and charged it to the GAME.

For years Fray had been trying to contain the monster thug that was desperately trying to re-emerge. When his mother died on him at the age of 13, *it was over!* Fray went wild and let the monster thug escape.

From age 13-to-19, Fray carried a *I don't give a fuck* attitude. It was *fuck you! Fuck your life! Fuck your wife! Fuck your kids! And fuck your mother!* During those wonder years Fray did so much dirt and committed so many murders that even Sadam Hussein would've been proud. Even jealous! All that work made Fray the street legend that he'd craved so much to become. It also made him the hunted. Another sibling living with Fray's grandmother in the Southwest section of D.C. tried to send him away to Florida with other relatives because she feared for his life but Fray ran away.

After a decade and some change of wilding out, Fray changed his ways and decided to get some Donald Trump money. Even the ordinary square could see the viscidity in his demeanor.

"I jive heard some shit about you, but I didn't know what you looked like." Flat-Head lied with the greatest of ease.

Truth be told, Flat-Head had been plotting on Fray for over two months, trying to learn all of his movements, in hopes of robbing him for his stash. When the two masked gunmen tried to beat Flat-Head to the prize, Flat-Head quickly decided to even the odds, in hopes of slithering into Fray's inner circle and securing his financial future.

"Where you from, Flat?"

"Over Linda Pollin," he answered, figuring that Fray was going to throw a couple kilos his way and tell him to take over Linda Pollin's drug market which was something he'd never do.

Flat-Head had no real intentions of ever selling drugs. He figured why waste time on the corner, ducking the LAW, when he could wait until the hustlers made the cash and take it from them?

"Oh Yeah? I fucked a few bitches over there, but anyway... Do you hustle?"

Naw, I kill and take niggas shit for a dollar. Flat-Head wanted to say, but he just looked at Fray and said, "I don't do no hand-to-hand shit on no corners. That shit is for them suckers... straight up!"

"A'ight, a'ight, my bad. Don't kill me, Flat." Fray chuckled, giving Flat-Head a sideward glance. But Flat-Head didn't laugh or respond.

Shawdy is on some straight serious time! Which is good in these evil streets. I like that. I like that alot. I'ma go ahead and fuck with shawdy on a major level. Fray thought, satisfied that he had a potential thorough soldier riding shotgun. Which is exactly what he'd been searching for.

Flat-Head caught Fray's slight smirk covering his face and wanted to know what was on the big-time hustler's mind. Flat-Head was convinced that Fray wasn't suspicious of him.

Satisfied that he'd slithered one step closer to Fray's riches, Flat-Head smiled from ear-to-ear, knowing that he'd just found the potential big payday that he had been searching for....

Chapter 6
Persuasion Through Seduction

At 4 p.m. that same day, Pepa found herself still hugged up with the handsome stranger, which was good news for her. Her goal was to gather as much information as she could on him and why he wanted to protect her.

Pepa knew men very well and she didn't expect him to fully open up to her without a little persuasion through seduction. Pepa backed up until she was rubbing her soft behind against him. When she felt the bulge in his shorts, Pepa knew her task would be easier than she'd thought.

At age 26, Pamela Sanders, also known as Pepa to her friends, looked like an innocent teenager, which was every man's fantasy. With an ass out of this world and a cute face to match, Pepa could easily crush any man's heart that she dealt with.

After losing her virginity to a perverted uncle at the tender age of 12, Pepa was determined to obtain the good life by using what her mother had given her. She watched pornographic films as if she was studying to obtain her master's degree. And she practiced vigorously to accomplish her goals of being a beast in bed. It paid off tremendously.

Over the past fourteen years Pepa had often fucked and sucked her way to a better lifestyle. It didn't matter if they were men or women. She despised all men for what her uncle had done to her and vowed to make all men pay for the countless sexual abuse she'd suffered.

Each time Pepa opened her legs to have sex she imagined each trick as if they were Shemar Moore, which was her favorite and sexiest man alive. So far her imagination worked, until today. Pepa didn't expect for the stranger in her house to resemble Shemar

Moore, and smell like Egyptian Musk cologne, which she loved smelling on a man.

By most of her tricks living outside of Valley Green projects, Pepa felt perfectly safe with her good girl reputation around The Valley. Besides, no man had ever knew where she lived, until today.

Pepa always knew dealing with guys in the streets would blow up in her face one day, but she never expected it to be this soon.

Pepa's thoughts of settling down with her Shemar Moore and watching him raise several kids that she birthed for him was like experiencing euphoria. Pepa realized she'd never forgive herself if she let the young stud get away from her. Her mind was made up.

As she turned over to face him and reached for the bulge in his shorts, Pepa felt a sense of rejuvenation, something that she hadn't felt in a very long time! Pepa felt like a woman again! She enjoyed the sensation that was washing over her. And at that moment Pepa knew it would only be a matter of time before she became Ramel's baby's mother! That sensation made her pussy wet....

Chapter 7
Who's Playing Who?

Ramel reacted to Pepa's advances like a little horny puppet. He knew that she was feeling him, but he didn't expect to fuck her so soon. Eventually he came to his senses, *once Pepa freed that swollen dick of his.*

"Hold up, Pepa. We can't rock like this," he stopped, then sat up and turned his back to her. *Go down you geekin' mothafucka!* Ramel told his dick, but it just ignored him. His dick was eagerly anticipating going swimming. Who could blame him? Pepa was a top flight bitch, who was ready to fuck!

Ramel figured if she was throwing the pussy at him this soon, then something wasn't right, unless she was a cold-blooded slut. *What is wrong with you?* He wondered, feeling her ease up on him.

"What's wrong, baby?" Pepa asked, massaging his shoulders, then kissing his neck, which he felt was apart of her plan to increase the seducing pressure on him. *To control me? Test my willpower?* He thought quizzically.

What is this bitch really up to? A bad bitch using seduction tactics? Starting a sex war? If a bad bitch like her can do this to a rack of men, why can't I do the same to all the bitches in the metropolitan area? All it would take is a crafty enough player with an ice cold heart. To pull it off, I can't catch feelings for women like Pepa. Ramel kicked to himself.

While Pepa kissed and massaged his back, Ramel realized his ticket to survival! The simple task of being able to turn a bitch out whenever he pleased. That made him see bright lights and huge bank accounts in his future.

25

At that moment Ramel remembered Mr. B's statement, "You're the architect of your destiny!" Ramel then made a silent vow to enjoy life to the fullest and it would be done off of the blood, sweat, and tears of all females.

"I just don't want to fuck up our budding friendship," he finally muttered. But something happened that made him lose all focus.

Pepa roughly pulled Ramel down on the bed and whispered, "You won't fuck up anything, but these tight pussy walls. We can be lovers and friends."

Before he could respond, Pepa had his throbbing dick in her small hands, stroking it lovingly. She stared at it, barely able to hide her appoving smile.

"I'ma treat you like you've never-ever been treated before." She huffed, closing her tiny fingers tightly around the base of his thickness.

"Don't make any promises that you can't keep." Ramel challenged.

She removed her skimpy skirt and eased out of her lemon-yellow thongs.

Pepa yanked down his shorts and boxers, and quickly dove head first for his love muscle.

"I always keep my promises, Ramel."

Kissing his pubic hairs and the tip of his dick, Pepa used both hands to slowly stroke him from the base to the tip. She was trying to measure the length.

"Don't keep playing with it. Gon' and show me what you working with," he urged as she looked up at him with a devilish grin and stretched her sultry lips to form an "O".

Pepa slowly took Ramel into her hot mouth inch by inch. His toes curled with the quickness, feeling her tongue-ring dance and glide across the bottom of his shaft. Once she got into a good rhythm, she turned her body until they were in a 69 position. Sitting her pussy on his face, Pepa began rubbing her wet pussy lips across his lips and nose. Ramel couldn't believe how good this top-ten model was deepthroating him, which made him want to return the favor, yet with more enthusiasm.

26

He looked up and stuck his nose in her slick slit, then snorted loudly. Ramel began lapping at her honey pot. The tangy taste of her wetness and the feeling of her hot-wet mouth on him was almost enough to make him explode.

He reached around and spread her soft ass cheeks so that he could lick her asshole also. When he made contact and tried to shove his tongue in her anus, he felt her shiver. Then warm liquid hit him in the chin and neck with the force of a spraying water gun.

"MMM...YESSS...OH MY GOD, Yesss... PUHleeassse don't stop. I, I just came like I've never came before, boy." She gasped, then went back to sucking him faster and faster.

Ramel began feeling that erupting point, "baby, hold up." Ramel moaned. But she just ignored him. Pepa deepthroated him and urged him to fuck her in the mouth until Ramel couldn't take no more.

"Pep... Pepa, girl you is a ba-beas---. AARRGGHHH!" He groaned, closing his eyes and jerking uncontrollably as his dick exploded in her mouth.

Pepa gripped Ramel's thighs and swallowed the babies from his spouting shaft.

Once she was sure she'd drained him, Pepa got off the bed and pulled off her halter-top and bra. She looked at him, smiling as if she had just found what she'd been missing her entire life.

Ramel wondered if she would still be smiling if she knew how old he was and the plans that he had in store for her?

She must've had dudes over here fucking her before, because she went straight to her burea and pulled out a box of condoms, Ramel thought to himself.

"Oh, it ain't over." She said, tossing him the rubber. "Put that on so I can keep my promise to you, boo."

While Ramel rolled on the condom he couldn't believe that his dick was still standing at attention. He guessed seeing Pepa laying on the bed playing with her pussy and moaning had a serious effect on him.

There was a slosh-slosh sound that her wet pussy made everytime she fingered herself.

"Mmmmm... You want some?" She asked seductively, while greedily sucking on her cunt-juice-coated fingers as if it was the best thing she'd ever tasted.

"Don't keep me waiting, boo." She moaned as Ramel's pulsing cock spasmed, streching the latex.

He wasted no time penetrating her soaking wet fuck-box. Ramel put her legs on his shoulders and pinched her clitoris roughly, while he drilled into her tight insides.

"AAAHH! AAHH!" She shrieked everytime he slammed in and out of her love tunnel.

Ramel watched her close her eyes, making ugly fuck-faces and biting her bottom lip. He pounded away roughly, making her perky breast sway up and down. He couldn't resist biting one of her pinkish-brown nipples.

When Pepa felt the carnal assault, her pussy spasmed, causing her walls to clench tightly on his stabbing shaft.

"YOU NASTY MOTHAFUCKA! OOOOHH, SHIT! AAAHH! AAAAAHHHH....AAAHH!" Her wails of ecstasy grew louder and louder as she bucked faster and faster to meet his thrust.

"I'M CA-CA-CUMMMINNNGGG!" She howled and he felt her ejaculate on his leg.

That shit blew his young mind!

This bitch skeeted like me! Ramel thought to himself, and it turned him on so much that he quickly followed. She wrapped her legs around his waist and held him inside of her until her legs began to tremble uncontrollably. His once massive love musle was now deflated. After the sexcapade they laid back in stunned silence. Several minutes passed before Pepa broke the quiet sound barrier.

"Did I keep my promise, boo?" She asked, kissing him on the neck.

The sex was mind-boggling, to say the least. Especially given the nature of how it got to that point. But Ramel couldn't let her know that. Then she would have the control, which was something that he couldn't allow.

"Not yet," he stated coldly. "I'm trying to figure out what's next? And how soon will it happen?"

Knowing that he'd just crushed her ego, Ramel began concentrating his attention on a close study of building her back up, which would hopefully lead him to her purse and eventually to her stash....

Chapter 8
A Snake In The Midst

Later that same afternoon, Fray and Flat were entering the Philadephia city limits. The city of Brotherly Love, as it's called. Fray was on a chill out mission from The District of Corruption's police, just in case somebody saw him committing murder and decided to snitch.

Lately, Fray's girlfriend, who attended Temple-U, had been complaining too much about his neglecting ways and how he wasn't spending time with her. Fray decided to pay her a visit and bring the young killer along, in hopes of introducing him to Philly, his home away from home. Philly was an interesting place to get paid, to say the least. A historical one, for better or worse.

Once they entered the foreign land, Flat-Head asked Fray where he was going.

"Over this lil' broad's house." Fray stated proudly, never knowing a snake was in his midst.

"So you doing it like that, huh?" Flat-Head quizzed, realizing there may have been more to this dude than he'd assumed.

"Listen Flat, you have to travel and politic. You can't stay cooped up in that city all your life. It's too damn small and everybody wants to be the man, which causes drama. Only two things can happen, you'll wind up with a thousand years in jail or end up in Harmony Cementary. That's why I spreads my shots. The key to this shit is them bitches. Find you a nice bitch in a couple of cities, then lock her down and investigate. Before you know it, you'll be moving in with your product. That's how them New Yorkers and Miami niggas did our town back in the '80's and early '90's." Fray pointed out.

"And most of them yammaz' went back home in a coffin! Straight up! Fuck them niggas! I stay on D.C. time, all the time!" Flat-Head stated saucily, knowing most of those out of towners had used the divide and conquer method, causing a rack of good men from D.C. to kill each other over the drugs that they were bringing into the city.

"I feel you scrap, but answer this. Where could you go right now if you were on the run? That town is too damn small."

"I see what you saying slim, but fuck that! Whatever happens is destiny anyway! Straight up!"

"You're absolutely right, because you're chilling with me Flat, and I'ma show you the fruits of what some serious hustling can bring." Fray said, navigating the Range Rover through the busy streets of North-Philly.

Flat-Head didn't respond. He decided to lay back, listen, learn, watch, and scheme. So when the opportunity presented itself he would be prepared for whatever.

It took three and a half months, but Flat had finally gotten closer to the prize and he was prepared to curl up and wait for as long as it took. He knew that his prey would slip up, giving him the perfect opportunity to strike....

Chapter 9
Brooke's Bitch?

There was more intrigue, or at least confusion, the following morning. According to what he'd heard off of the early morning wake up. Pepa had called Ramel from the kitchen and told him to *get out*.

"WHAT?" he yelled in disbelief. They'd had sex all night and he'd tried to break his dick off in the bitch! Was this the kind of thanks he was going to get?

"You heard me! I have to go somewhere, boy!" Was all she said.

The assumptions that Ramel had of Pepa was already wrong and fucking with his mental. It was possible that he'd misjudged her, but he didn't know if he could believe it. Ramel had always called money on women, but this time he hit rock bottom!

After he showered, dressed, and got ready to leave, Pepa was in the living room with some girl. The two of them were huddled together on the sofa, conspiring about *only God knew what*. Ramel was a little suspicious as to why Pepa's girlfriend was there so early in the morning.

"Pepa, what's really happening?" he asked. "It's like that, huh?"

"Like what, Ramel?" She sucked her teeth as if she was irritated.

"Don't play with me. Whose this?" he looked at the dark-chocolate female, whose jeans looked like they were going to burst at the seams if she moved too much. Imagine looking at a dark skin version of Alicia Keys with a Buffie The Body frame! That shit was way too serious for a young nigga!

"Brooke was in the neighborhood. She just came to see me and take me shopping." Pepa answered, which gave Ramel a little hope, because the bitch didn't owe him any explanations. By her explaining, he could sense she was feeling him, or so he thought.

"Well actually," Brooke spoke up. "My girl was feeling a little bad and shopping cheers her up. So I decided to come and take her."

"Damn bitch! Why not just scream all of my business out." Pepa scolded, sucking her teeth.

Brooke nodded and smiled pleasantly before sighing out loud.

Ramel had no idea what all this was about. Yet the sight of all that pussy in Brooke's jeans caused him to smile also as he leaned back onto the couch.

"If you don't tell him I will, Pepa."

"Damn, I hate you sometimes." Pepa said, rolling her demon-green eyes, then looking at Ramel.

"Ramel, Brooke stays here. And, well, she's my lover....I'm sorry."

"And what does that shit have to do with me?" Ramel asked, giving Brooke's lesbian-ass a challenging look.

Brooke smiled triumphantly and shook her head. "Nothing actually. She was just giving you the heads up about me. She told me all about how you stayed here with her last night and looked after her after that shooting demo. Now that I'm home, you can go. Thanks for all that you've done though."

This smart ass bitch doesn't even have a clue that I blew her girlfriend's back out all night! Dumb-ass bitch. I should blackmail this freak-ass bitch. Ramel thought, glancing at Pepa, who was giving him a "Please don't say nothing," pleading look.

"I can respect that Ms. Brooke, but time is money. Since I lost about $1,500 by baby-sitting your girl here, don't you feel that I should be compensated for my services?" Ramel asked, staring directly at Pepa. He didn't give a fuck where

33

the blackmail ransom came from, just as long as it was paid.

All I have is $900, you lil' crook! Even though the dick is big and good, it's not worth no damn $1,500! It's suppose to be vise-versa muthafucka! Pepa wanted to yell, but remained quiet from fear of slipping up in front of her longtime lover, and exposing her infidelities.

It was during the latter part of '96 when Pepa met Brooke, whom inculcated her to step her *hustling-men game* up, and eventually became Pepa's lover. It was Brooke who taught Pepa the true meaning of Love & Loyalty.

Although they were both caught up in sexing men for money, they always found time to take care of home. Brooke and Pepa never wanted for anything. They just became addicted to chasing and doing shit for the love of money.

"Boy, you outta your fucking mind!" Brooke snapped, drawing Pepa out of her reverie. "Don't nobody got no $1,500 laying around here. Boy, lemme' get some of that shit that you been smoking on."

Hearing her sarcasm made Ramel mad, but he didn't show it. He simply shook his head at them and said, "You got way more than $1,500 worth of shit up in here. So let me get something."

"FUCK NO!" Brooke yelled, then glared at Ramel evilly.

Brooke had a mean spirit and he could tell she was far from a pushover, but fuck that! He was not leaving there empty-handed.

"Have it your way, sexy," he stated, looking at Pepa, who was fidgeting and bouncing her legs up and down rapidly. Ramel knew that she was hella' nervous.

"Don't get me started about the number of same sex relationships in this city that falls apart because of in--"

"Listen Ramel," Pepa cut in. "I can give you a little something now, and the rest next week."

"What-the-fuck-ever! Just get his ass up outta here!" Brooke snarled and stood up from the couch to leave.

Ramel jive liked Brooke's sexy ass. And to be honest, it was because he felt a little intimidated by her. Why was that? Ramel wondered as Pepa handed him some cash. It was $500! Not bad at all for his first sting on a bitch.

It was at that point that he noticed Brooke's hour-glass frame. She stood about 5'7". With all of that body, it was a shame that she was letting it go to waste by not getting the proper dick nourishment. Truth be told, she looked even better than Pepa. Ramel was almost embarrassed to have noticed.

"What the fuck is you staring at?" Brooke spat, sucking her teeth, which irritated the fuck out of him.

"Nothing really." Ramel protested. Suddenly he didn't want to leave. Ramel wanted to talk about something instead of bickering and arguing.

"Well, look at nothing on your way out the door," she fired back and walked away.

When she was gone, he heard the bedroom door slam and Pepa shoved him roughly.

"Why you tried to fuck up a happy home? You're cruddy as shit, you know that?" She hissed.

"Maybe I am," he grinned and shrugged. "But I'm not as cruddy as your nasty-cheating-good-pussy ass."

"Fuck you!" She said, then kissed him with obvious affection. "You take care of that dick for me... Don't forget to come back and see me next week."

"Is you asking me? Or telling me?" Ramel quizzed.

"What do you think?" She asked back.

"I think you're full of secrets. Why you ain't tell me that you was dyking?"

Pepa frowned and raised an eyebrow at him.

"Maybe it's because you never asked me. Maybe because it's none of your business. Maybe it's because I want my cake and ice cream. Why ask why Ramel? You know I charge niggas $500 or better for what you got from me last night. And your cruddy ass turn around and charged me. You know, you could just be the one man for me, and that scares me, which is a good thing."

Ramel thought about it. He really didn't have a response. It had been a long tiresome night, and a crazy confusing morning. His brain wasn't clicking on all channels yet.

"I'm about to roll, Pepa. You sure you don't want me to stay?" he asked, reaching for her crotch area. It looked like a camel's toe in those form-fitting jeans she had on.

"Ramel, stop playing!" Pepa smiled, slapping his hand away. "When I need you again, I know how to reach you, more or less." She said, then kissed him on the lips and escorted him to the front door.

"It's gonna cost you too, more or less." Ramel turned and chirped over his shoulder.

Pepa smiled and closed the door.

As Ramel left Pepa's apartment, he realized it was indeed him against the world. He had to use everything that he had to get what he wanted from that day forward.

Unbeknownest to Pepa and Ramel, Brooke was ear-hustling and had heard every painful word of their conversation....

Chapter 10
Snakes Think Alike

Meanwhile, somewhere in the North Philly area, Fray parked at the corner of Tenth and Brown Street. He was in a rented black Dodge Magnum, watching his latest vic' enter the apartment complex.

Fray's hustle was hooking up with drug dealers from out of town and selling the product in D.C. Once he earned their trust, Fray would reveal his snake-like ways, and rob them blind. Now that he had a thoroughbred with him, Fray figured he could step his game up.

Fray and Flat were dressed in blue repairmen coveralls, efficiently blending in with the morning crew of maintenance workers that took care of the apartment complex. They wore gloves, baseball caps, and small white dust protector masks around their necks for easy access. They could easily raise them to conceal their facial features.

When Fray put Flat on point about how he'd been buying weight and chilling with Shabazz -- a big time hustler/Muslim -- for over ten months just to rob him, Flat knew he'd stumbled onto some major caper type shit.

All this time I've been plotting on this nigga and he's doing the same shit to the out of towners? Just my type of guy, Flat thought as Fray brought him up to speed on how he'd familiarized himself with Shabazz's rountine of dumping off kilos and collecting money. The Richard Allen Projects in North Philly was Shabazz's last stop before heading home to his condo in Loyola Merion. He shared the condo with a sexy Philladephia 76er's cheerleader.

"Your shit is way serious Fray. Straight up!"

"I told you, I'ma show you what some serious hustling can get you. Just think, in a few more minutes, you're gonna have more money than you ever seen in yo' life." Fray said just as Shabazz exited the apartment building, jumped in an old Ford Exoline van and pulled off.

"That's what he drops the coke off in." Fray pointed out, slowly pulling out into the early morning traffic. Shabazz was oblivious to what lurked behind him. Once a light-weight hustler, Shabazz had stepped his game up to the point where Fray had heard about him. And that's all it took to attract the wolf!

Fray waited until the van got a few cars ahead before he relaxed and followed at a safe distance. Flat-Head was loading his weapon with .45 caliber Rhino-Heads slugs, and wondering what his man Ramel was doing. Flat mentally went over the killing he'd done yesterday, making sure that Ramel was in the clear of any criminal activity. Once he was satisfied, Flat-Head shifted back to the task at hand.

I know a few jokers outta state that's pushing keys of powder/ Time to make a withdrawal / Let me get that coward... If you buck, then you fucked, I'm sending you to immortal ground / If you wanna live follow my orders, and gimme' the loot now / It's GOING DOWN... Flat-Head quickly put together four bars in his head. He intended to put them in his book of rhymes later.

Besides thuggin' to the fullest, Flat-Head's other passion was writing gritty rap songs. Flat wanted to become the first major rap star out of D.C. To do that, Flat felt he had to come up with enough start up capital to put his indepenant record label together. Then he'd make his dream come true.

"He's stopping at some gas station now." Fray said, breaking into Flat-Head's thoughts. "That's why niggas always get got, because they don't know how to switch they style up."

With that said, Fray drove past the gas station and parked at a discreet distance from the condominum complex. Once they saw the van cruise pass them and park in the complex, Flat and Fray eased out of the car and trotted towards Shabazz's building. It was relatively early, and both thugs looked like people that worked on the complex's grounds, so none of the neighbors paid them any attention.

Once they entered Shabazz's building, Fray signaled Flat to put on his mask and get ready for whatever …

Chapter 11
Why You Hate Me?

"Give that shit up, nigga! You know what time it is! Don't turn this robbery into a homicide." Ramel heard the threat and couldn't believe his luck.

I just pulled a caper on a bitch and it came back to bite me in the ass this quick? Why do you hate me so much Lord? Why me? He thought as the gun-wielding man with a red bandanna covering his dark face ordered him to empty his pockets.

"You got that, slim. Just don't buss' me." Ramel muttered, trembling a little. There was absolutely no faking, he was scared as shit! Ramel knew plenty of dudes who got killed that way, and he damn sure didn't want to join them! Not yet, anyway.

"What! Who the fuck is you talking to? HUH?" The jacker barked, aiming the gun recklessly.

"Na-nobody. Here you go! That's everything I got, slim." Ramel lied, passing him the $500. He had $250 stashed in his shoe and it was the only thing he had left besides his name and the clothes on his unlucky ass.

"Shut yo' bitch-ass up!" the gunman growled, snatching the money from Ramel. "Is you from around her, bitch-nigga?"

"Naw, I'm from over Linda Pollin."

"I can't stand them punks anyway. Never did like ya'll fake ma'fuckas!" He griped, raising the chunky pistol to Ramel's chest level, looking directly into his eyes.

Seeing his finger tighten around the trigger, Ramel's eyes widened in horror. But he didn't wait around to see if the man would pull the trigger or not.

Soon as Ramel turned and took off sprinting, the Linda Pollin hating lunatic began letting loose with the deadly weapon. The explosions were deafening in the dark hallway. Ramel could smell the acrid odor of gunpowder. Dude sure as shit wasn't doing no faking!

What happened next was a blur. Ramel heard three more explosions, and saw the ground rushing up to punch him in the face and body.

Slamming on the dirty tiles, it felt like he'd been hit by a Mack Truck at full speed. Ramel began crawling rapidly and yelling for help.

"HEEELLLPP ME! SOMEBODY, PUHLEEASSE HELP MEEE!" he wailed, struggling to reach Pepa's apartment door. Ramel looked back and noticed that the crazed gunman was gone, which was a relief. Ramel didn't want to die just yet. He knew that hot-balls had torn into him because he was getting weak, and he could see the trail of blood behind him. Ramel's whole body was on fire!

Reaching Pepa's door, he banged on it with all of the strength that he could muster.

When nobody answered, Ramel cried like a two-year old. And for the first time during this whole event, he actually feared for his life. He didn't want to die alone in some dark hallway in the projects.

He wanted to live and build his destiny. Feeling life slowly slip away Ramel thought about all he'd never done in life, and knew that he couldn't just give up.

"PEPA! PUHLEEASSSE GOD! PEPA, IF YOU CARE ABOUT LIFE AT ALL, THEN OPEN THE DOOR, PUHLEEASSSE!" he yelled, feeling his eyes closing involuntarily.

Ramel tried to stay conscious as the sounds of the door unlocking got louder, but it just wasn't happening.

He started coughing and began choking on his own blood. Faintly he heard someone yelling, " RAMEL! OH MY GOD! RAMEL! HOLD ON, BABY! DON'T YOU DIE ON ME!"

Ramel continued to struggle for each breath. Then reality hit. At that moment he realized that he may have disappointed whoever was yelling for him to live.

His eyelids slammed shut, feeling as if they weighed a ton. Ramel drifted away as he was being lifted on an ambulance gurney. He couldn't believe it. His destiny was to get shot on that day and he never saw it coming. From there everything went black....

Chapter 12
Ock' Slippin' On His Pimpin'

MEANWHILE, BACK ON THE OUTSKIRTS OF WEST PHILLY, Shabazz had just reached his building with two duffel bags when his light-brown eyes regarded the two men dressed in maintenance worker's garb. They appeared out of nowhere with a certain guarded suspicion.

Shabazz dropped the duffel bags and reached for his pistol. Before Shabazz got his hands on it, Fray tackled him as if he were the Pro-Bowl linebacker Brian Urlacher stopping Micheal Vick on 4th and goal for the game winning touchdown.

Flat-Head moved quickly behind Fray, taking the Glock-45 from Shabazz's waist. He then looked at Fray.

"Take them bags to the car and get back her a-sap!" Fray ordered.

Flat did as he was instructed. Fray shoved the gun into Shabazz's side and told him to get up real slow.

Once he was up, Fray walked Shabazz down the hallway to the last condominium on the right. When Shabazz noticed that his assailant already knew where to go, he figured the guy had been watching him for quit some time.

How in the fuck did I get caught slipping like this? Shabazz scolded himself as Fray instructed him to open the door.

"C'mon Ock', it ain't got to be this--"

Shabazz's pleading words were cut short by a sharp blow to the head from Fray's pistol.

"It is what it is, nigga! Now open up the got-damn door!" Fray snarled, jabbing the gun harder against Shabazz's rib cage.

Shabazz complied, leading Fray inside his lavishly

decorated condo, just as Flat was returning to the scene. Once Flat got inside the condo, he closed the door and produced two rolls of duct tape.

"Lay the fuck down, young bull." Fray mimicked the Philly native's slang so Shabazz wouldn't think to seek revenge outside of Philly.

"Tie his ass up, Ock'." Fray ordered and Flat-Head began taping Shabazz's wrists and ankles together while Fray held him at gunpoint.

Feeling the wads of duct tape cover his mouth, Shabazz's anger began boiling over behind the huge loss he was about to take. More importantly, Shabazz was thinking about his girlfriend, Layla, who was in the bedroom sound asleep. Shabazz began praying that the robbers would just take the money and run.

"Ay yo, the bitch told me that the safe was in the hallway linen closet. I'm 'bout to see if my pimp hand is official." Fray stated, watching Shabazz's eyes widen.

When Shabazz heard that he felt betrayed. Nobody knew about that safe, but one person. The slut who was sleeping in his bed. The same slut who had tricked him to fall in love with her.

Shabazz made a silent vow to kill her once he made it through the traumatizing ordeal. Once again life had taught him a costly learning experience.

"Yo Ock, I'ma check the bedroom for anything out of order." Fray said as Flat aimed the Glock-45 at Shabazz's forehead.

"A'ight, I'ma watch this nut ass nigga while you do you."

Once Fray disappeared, Flat-Head decided to have a little fun at the victim's expense.

"Hey, my man." Flat whispered. "If you give me a million dollars right now, I'll get you out of here. I know you want to live and get some type of revenge, Ock?"

Shabazz quickly turned his head away from Flat, which made Flat-Head feel disrespected.

"Fine then. Have it your way, you bitch ass nigga!" Flat

43

growled. Then he began smacking Shabazz with the pistol that he'd just taken from him. Flat showed him that he was the wrong nigga to ignore.

Blood started spurting from the fresh gashs in the prey's head. Flat found it hilarious. He couldn't hold it in. Flat-Head howled with uncontrollable laughter, before hearing an ear-shattering scream from the bedroom....

$ $ $

"Shut up, bitch! I told you that I was coming to see you didn't I?" Fray chuckled as the startled woman tried to pull the covers over her naked figure.

"Fray, I--"

"Fray my ass, Layla." Fray hissed, cutting her off and causing her to flinch from him.

Layla Collins was a curvaceous honey-toned beauty in her late twenties. She had an abundance of charm and a deceptively naive manner. Beneath the good looks and alluring body lurked a devious woman who knew about the power of PUSSY inside and out. Layla was a woman who could sweet talk a pimp out of some money, because she could fuck like nobody else and then stab a mu'fucka in the back without a second thought.

Layla was a deadly snake, like Fray, which was why the two of them got along so well, until now!

Layla started her illustrious street career fucking for Reeboks, moved on to Gold-Digging, and then wifey material. Along the way she broke a few hearts, eventually catching the attention of a Philadephia 76ers B-Ball star, who single-handedly championed her rise to Captain of the cheerleading squad. Some said that her and Eric Snow were lovers. Fray didn't believe it one bit and was too smart to try and reel her in like all the other male groupies. Fray paced himself, managing to show up at the same places and gatherings that Layla attended several times a month. At which times they began speaking and exchanged information, because they genuinely liked each other.

"What's up, moe?" Flat-Head asked, invading Fray's thoughts after bursting in the bedroom and spotting the naked female.

"Ain't shit." Fray said, grabbing a handful of Layla's auburn hued mane and pulling her out of the large circular bed.

"I just have to check my bitch, you dig? She tried to sneak away and play without paying attention to her moves. Always watch them hookers, because they try to pull a fast one on you real quick." Fray said as Layla hit the floor with a sickening thud.

"Ba-baby, I can explain!" Layla cried.

"Save that shit, hoe! You slipped up and fell on the dick, huh? I told you that *what I don't know will hurt you!* But bitch you don't believe shit stinks, huh?"

Flat-Head openly stared at the naked woman and began backing out of the bedroom, but Fray stopped him.

"Don't go nowhere, scrap. This bitch is a pure-D-slut, so I'ma treat her like one." Fray snarled, tracing Layla's round and full pretty breasts with the barrel of his gun.

When Fray reached the curly pubic hairs between Layla's thick light-brown thighs, Flat-Head's dick stiffened quickly.

Damn, this Fray's bitch? She's too bad to be a slut like that. I wonder what she did to make him so mad at her? Flat thought, watching Fray roughly grip her by her hair.

"So you wanna be a freak, huh?"

"NO!" She cried.

"Yes you do, bitch! I caught you red handed. Ay', c'mere, moe."

Flat walked over to the bed as Fray smacked Layla ferociously, then picked her up and threw her back onto the bed. Fray quickly taped her wrists together, then rolled her onto her flat stomach.

"Go ahead and dig in, slim. She got some good pussy." Fray smirked, looking at his new crime partner.

Layla couldn't believe her ears! What was Fray about to have done to her? He'd claimed that he loved her. But he did warn her to never hurt him. Still, that didn't give him the right to tell a complete stranger to *go ahead and fuck her!*

45

Like their two and a half year relationship meant nothing to him.

Fueled by anger and fear, Layla went wild and began struggling to break free, but both men's strength was too much for her.

"Move again, here, and I'ma fuck you up for real!" Fray threatened as Flat dropped his coveralls and forced her thick legs apart.

Fray placed the pistol against Layla's temple while Flat-Head's rigid cock penetrated her warm fuck-hole.

"NOOO! PUHLEEEAASSEE, FRAY! TELL HIM TO STOPPP! WHY ARE YOU DOING THIS TO MEEE!" Layla yelled, feeling the stranger's dick slam roughly into her sacred center from behind. Realizing that she was being raped per order of the man she once loved, and that she couldn't do anything to stop it. At one point in time Layla would have jumped in front of a speeding bullet for Fray, to prove her love for him. Now she felt violated, sick, and betrayed by him. She now viewed him as a heartless monster.

"Shut up bitch!" Fray smacked her again. Flat-Head's fuck pole drilled her vigorously, enjoying the feel of her tight warm pussy.

"I'ma teach you a serious lesson about crossing me!" Fray snarled as Flat gripped her small waist and pulled her back to meet his animalistic strokes.

"AAAAAAHHHHHH! STOPPPP IT! STOPPP!" Layla cried, causing Flat to speed up his pace. He was getting excited by her screams.

After close to ten minutes of rough-house fucking, Flat exploded inside of Layla, extracted his limp penis and pulled up his coveralls. Soon as Flat-Head was done, Fray snatched Layla off the bed and took her out of the bedroom. Flat quickly picked up his gun and followed them.

Once in the hallway, Layla began pleading to Fray for him to stop dogging her out.

"Tell me why should I, bitch?" Fray growled.

"Because I da-did all of this shit for you. You told me to

46

do this, Fray." She sniffled.

"If you loved me, you would've never agreed to no sick ass shit like this. That's where you failed the test, shawdy." Fray said, fucking her up mentally more than ever.

The rape was one thing, but that last remark took the cake! Oh hell no! He's not getting away with this shit! Layla thought to herself.

"You know what Fray, I use to love the ground you walked on, now I despise it. And you know what else?" She smiled before continuing. "I hate you, bitch!" Layla blustered and spat in Fray's face. "AND I HOPE YOU DIE, BITCH!"

"Tell me something that no other broad has told me!" Fray fired back smiling; then wiped the globs of saliva from his face.

Flat-Head watched all of the drama unfold, itching to pull his trigger. He wasn't use to seeing any females spit on a street dude without catching some serious backlash, like an ass whipping or some hot lead for the blatant disrespect.

"I hope your slut ass die quicker!" Fray muttered, placing his gun to Layla's forehead. He then kissed her on the lips and squeezed the trigger twice, causing Shabazz and Flat to flench from the sudden explosion of gunfire.

Fray's coveralls were painted with Layla's blood as he let her lifeless body crumbled to the floor. Fray calmly walked to the linen closet and removed the four foot sheet metal safe.

"Spit out the combination and you'll live," was all Fray said.

Flat roughly snatched the duct tape off of Shabazz's mouth.

"Fuck ya'll pussy-ass niggas. I'm not spitting out shi--"

Flat-Head silenced Shabazz with two shots to the head, causing Fray to scream, "NOOOOOOO, FLAT-HEAD, DAMN!"

"Fuck that nigga! Straight up!" Flat said and began shooting at the safe. To Fray's surprise the door slowly cracked open.

"See how easy that was? We ain't need his punk ass." Flat said, then rushed towards the safe.

47

They ran around the condo grabbing several pillowcases with intentions of emptying the safe and making an unnoticeable escape before the FEDS showed up. They figured somebody had probably called 9-1-1 and reported hearing gunshots fired.

"Let's move, nigga!" Fray urged as Flat quickly stuffed the last of the four pillowcases filled with money and drugs and fled the condo. Leaving two dead bodies for the cops to ponder over.

Once they reached the rental car, Fray went off on Flat-Head.

"Muthafucka', don't you ever fuck up a sweet lick like that!" He blustered. "I was gonna let the chump live, so I could get his ass again."

"You should've told me that shit from the jump. Straight up! So whose the one that really fucked up the sweet lick?" Flat asked, pulling out his extra gun and placing it on his lap.

"You needs to ease up with all that press to kill shit, Flat. I'm serious."

"Look whose talking, Mr. Smashing My Girlfriend after ordering *her to be raped-ass nigga.* You're the one that's fucked up, moe! Straight up!" Flat-Head said and they both howled with laughter.

As Fray calmly made a quick getaway, he was still in a semi state of shock and disbelief from witnessing Flat-Head's sudden rape and kill with no signs of remorse.

They'd been forced to leave behind alot more money and drug, because the safe had been filled to capacity.

Fray respected Flat-Head's go hard mentality, but he could tell that Flat couldn't think pass go.

Shawdy's a loose cannon and that's a plus for me, because I can let him loose on all them sucker, and reap the benefits. But I also have to watch his ass, because he's big headed and one of those type of niggas that doesn't give a fuck about who he kills to get ahead in life. And I can't see myself getting tricked by a wild-juvenile, who hasn't seen nor done half the shit that I've done in life, Fray thought as he headed

48

towards the downtown Marriot....

Chapter 13
Am I Dead?

Am I dead? If I am, where am I? Ramel asked himself.

It was pitch black and freezing cold. Very scary and disorienting, to put it mildly. No lights anywhere. *Is this part of the Creator's plan? What is supposed to happen to me next? Where am I headed? And Why?* He continued to question the situation at hand.

Ramel tried to collect his thoughts and make a rough plan to navigate his way through the afterlife, for the next eternity at least, in a semi organized manner. Difficult to do, maybe impossible. Ramel was searching for the light that seemed to have vanished, to have been gobbled up by the darkness. All-the-while searching for that voice that begged him to hold on, not to die. *Why would they want me to live?* It just didn't make sense. Nothing made sense so far. Especially the state of limbo that he was currently stuck in.

"Sow him up and send him to recovery," he faintly heard someone say. And shortly after he was moving, hoping to see that light again that he really missed. It seemed like a long shot, but Ramel didn't have anything else. He was moving faster, then suddenly he stopped. He didn't want to miss this -- whatever was about to happen!

"My baby! Oh thank you, doctor. Thank you Sweet Jesus. You saved my baby's life," he heard his mother say. Her voice sounded full of relief and joy. "When can I take him home?"

"We have to run some test," then the doctor's words seemed to go.

Tuning out their conversation and his surroundings, he began thinking about Pepa, trying once again to figure out what could possibly tie her to the shit that he found himself in... the disaster that ended with an attempt on his life.

"Who was she working with?" he wondered.

One thing was clearly obvious and probably useful to him; he knew where she lived.

"Ramel, can you hear me, baby? This is your mother," she said softly, then touched his hand. "Baby, if you can hear me, I just want you to know that I'm so sorry for pushing you away. If I could take back the last twenty four hours, believe me baby, I would, but I can't. Ramel, I love you and I want to see you do better than that useless shit out there in them streets. That's the only reason why I was so hard on you. Baby, I want to see you succeed."

From that moment on, there was very little that he could do but listen and learn. As she poured her heart out to him about how she met his Pops in the streets and did things that she now regretted. Things that she wasn't proud of. It infuriated him because she was trying to run from her past. Such a hypocrite!

Ramel had heard that *your past always predicted your future.* So he began wondering if his future would be full of darkness and pain, like his present?

"Baby, Mama promise from now on, I'll try to be more understanding of your fast-ass ways. Like it or not, you are coming back home. Even if I have to send you away for awhile, you're coming back home. I rather have you hating me and alive under my roof, than me hating myself forever, knowing that I failed you as a mother."

Her words shot down his ears like a lear jet shooting down an airport runway, then going airborne. *Could she know that I was there, hearing every word? Could she know the level of tension and frustration that I was feeling just increased courtesy of her words? Could she know I wanted to die just to escape her tormenting way?* He further questioned.

Just then he began to wander deep into the dark abyss, where it was very nice and quiet. Much, much better than hearing her bullshit.

Then the quiet was broken. The light quickly returned and

51

he saw and heard Pepa, his mother and two detectives discussing the attempt on his life. And even though he was happy to see and breathe again, Ramel panicked by the sight of the police, and the thought of them asking him anything....

Chapter 14
The Bitch Tried To Kill Me?

A FEW DAYS LATER, Ramel woke up to Brooke pushing a pillow over his face. She was trying to kill him.

"Die bitch!" Brooke hissed as he struggled to keep her from suffocating him.

The oxygen pumping from his lungs were like oil gushing from an open well. *Why is this bitch trying to kill me?* His mind raced for answers.

He tried to scream as his eyes opened wide with fear, knowing what would come next if he didn't stop her. When Ramel opened his mouth, the heavy pillow muffled his screams.

Then Brooke struck again! The viscious blows connected to his ribs.

Once!

Twice!

Three times she punched him where he'd been shot and operated on.

"GGRRrrr..." he groaned a horrible death rattle of a groan, and within seconds he remembered the emergency call button by his side. It would alert the nurse's station if he could only get to it.

Ramel ceased struggling and searched the bed for the button with his hands. He felt lightheaded as she applied more force to the pillow. His lungs screamed for air and the only way to get it was to find the button.

"Where is it!?!"

"I'ma kill you mothafucka!" She hissed while Ramel began shaking, still searching for the button and feeling weaker by the second.

"BINGO, I GOT ACTION!" his mind released as his finger found its target.

Soon as he touched it, he began pressing it rapidly. Seconds passed before he heard that wonderful high pitch bleeping sound that used to irritate the hell out of him. Now it became music to his ears. The next thing Ramel knew the pillow's pressure suddenly eased up.

"It ain't over, boy!" Brooke snarled as he knocked the pillow from his face. Breathing erractically, he saw Brooke sitting on the edge of the hospital bed, poking holes in his I.V. tubes.

"What the fuck ain't over?" he probed breathlessly. "Bitch, you just tried to kill me!"

"I know that you fucked Pepa. So if you really want her bad enough, then you have to die for her. Are you ready to go all out over her? I know I am ready to die for my girl."

"Bitch, you is crazy!"

"Only crazy about my Pepa," she grinned maniacally with a saucy wink. "Let this be a warning to you. Pepa's mines, so stay the fuck away from her," she murmured sweetly, tucking him in bed like a mother would do her child.

"If you don't, I promise I will make your life a living hell to remember."

Before Ramel could object, Brooke was on her feet and backing away. She stared at him with an *I dare you* smile. That shit really scared the shit out of him. When she slipped out of the door he breathed a sigh of relief.

That bitch is crazy! She won the battle, but I'm going to win the war! That's on my dead Pop and my brother.

Several nurses rushed in the room, checking his vital signs. Ramel shook his head, not quite believing what was happening to him. He wasn't used to a woman trying to kill him over a piece of pussy!

He was shocked and infuriated. *How did Brooke find out that we had sex? Had Pepa told her? Was Brooke just warning me to stay away? Or was she really trying to kill me?* Ramel shivered at the thought!

Chapter 15
So What?

BROOKE GUISHARD THOUGHT OF herself as an in control and reasonable woman, but in view of what had happened over the last 48 hours, she couldn't remain calm. Her faithful partner, lover and best friend had betrayed her; and it infuriated Brooke that Pepa had lied and cheated on her in such a way. *The disloyal son-of-a-bitch.*

Brooke stood under the powerful jets of the hotel suite's shower, soaking her body. After what she'd just done at the hospital, she felt the need to thoroughly cleanse herself of all her sins. Disloyalty and dishonesty disgusted her no matter what form it came in.

Last night Brooke felt like the world as she knew it was coming to an end. She knew she had to get out of the apartment and away from Pepa. She had no desire to lie in bed beside Pepa, listening to her cry over Ramel, hoping that he'd live through the shooting.

"Damn Pep', you act like you're fucking him." Brooke snapped, releasing some pent up anger. After easedropping earlier, she was trying to find a way to bring up the subject of what she'd overheard.

"Don't even go there, Brooke." Pepa said irritably, sucking her teeth, which made Brooke angrier.

"I'm already there! Did you fuck him?" She asked, already knowing the answer. She wanted to see if Pepa would lie or come clean.

"Yeah, so what?" Pepa snapped, wondering why her girlfriend was nagging her about the same things they'd done to make a good fortune and lived well off of.

"Yeah, so what?" Brooke mimicked saucily. "Bitch, you know we had an understanding! Business is business, and that's all we fuck niggas for, business! You just did the mothafuckin' opposite. What, you were trying to hide the fact that you fucked him? Don't even answer." Brooke held up a hand and got out of bed. "Bitch, I hate you! I'm outta here. And I hope that mothafucka does croak!"

"BITCH, I HATE YOU!" Was all Brooke heard echoing from Pepa's voice while she grabbed a few belongings.

Brooke couldn't stomach hearing about Pepa's betrayal, so she left the apartment deeply disturbed and hurt by Pepa's infidelity.

I'm tired of her shit. I thought she loved me? What the hell is up with her? Don't she realize how good I am to her? Maybe one day she'll recognize what she has in me and give me all of her love and loyalty. Brooke thought to herself.

Brooke wanted to scream and cry out. Yell her undying love for Pepa. But no, she couldn't do that. Not right now. She felt she had to stay mentally strong for her visit with Ramel.

And strong she'd remained, all the way down to Ramel alerting the nurses with that stupid emergency button. *Why I didn't think of looking for that contraption?* She thought, realizing she almost killed a man to proclaim her love for Pepa, *a no good slut.*

Even though she was mad at Pepa and felt like a fool for going after Ramel, Brooke knew she would do it again if someone ever touched Pepa, *outside of the realms of business*…But someone had touched her. And all she could say was *so what*…

Chapter 16
Life Ain't Fair?

PROPPED UP IN THE HOTEL SUITE'S KING SIZE BED, watching the hood classic film, STREET RAISED, Flat-Head was completely comfortable and feeling so good; thanks to the miracle of Purpla Haze and some oral sex.

All of the Philly women that they met turned out to be fans and groupies. Well, how often was it that they got their hands on a genuine GO-Hard nigga from D.C.? They kept flirting and freely offering to go back to his hotel room just to take a shot at him and ask a few questions like: *Did he know Wayne Perry or the leader of Murder Inc., Kevin Gray? Was the city really dangerous and rough to live in? Or was it just portrayed that way for the public outside of the city?* Simple questions that inquiring minds outside of D.C. wanted answers to.

Over the last 72 hours, Flat-Head got off on being the center of attention and having sex with several gorgeous women from Philly. Now he had his eyes on the bobbing head of the pretty naked brown-skin woman who possessed a Beyonce superstar quality about her. He loved her oral skills, not to mention her soft ass and full C-cup sized breasts. Flat had met her earlier while shopping with Fray at the Gallery Mall. Fray had her best friend in the suite next door, fucking her brains out. She told Fray that she wanted to get double penetrated by them as soon as her friend went to sleep.

Yes, all in all, Flat felt that it wasn't all that bad leaving D.C. Because now Fray was completely blind to his hidden agenda, which he felt was a good thing.

Soon as I get back to The City, I'm back on cruddy time

57

as usual. At first I was going to let Fray punk-ass get away. But after he gave me $100,000 out of all that shit we got from that caper, it's a must that I rob his petty ass, he thought and kept curling his toes and palming the woman's bobbing head as she deepthroated him quite pleasantly.

I might have to keep in touch with this bitch, Flat thought, watching as she quickly straddled him and inserted his tubesteak inside her wet oven.

Boom, his eyes closed. He was in heaven again, which was how her pussy made him feel.

"Mmmm...Gimme that dick, Daddy." She purred, bucking on him until she got a fast rhythm going. "Don't slow down on me now.... Fuck this pussy...MMMmmmmmmmm."

"Never that! Straight up!" He mumbled, slamming her down on his impaling sword. She took every inch of his invading love.

"Your friend to-told me...Mmmm...That you're la-looking for a place ta-ta-to...Mmmm...Looking for a place to stay... you know, when you come up Philly to chill." She moaned, licking her own nipples while she bounced up and down on his jabbing piston like she was riding a wild bull. "I may ca-can help you out!"

"You may can help...or you will help, Mya?"

"I'll do whatever you wa-want, if you keep ga-going until you buss my ga-ga-G-Spot." Mya moaned, licking her lips and raising her pelvis bone away from his in an effort to savor the thickness of his juicy shaft. She loved how it stretched her pussy walls.

"Oh yeah?" Flat beamed, putting his arms around Mya's shoulders and pulling her exquisite hour-glass frame down on his impaling shaft.

Mya tried to sit up and ride him like she loved doing, but sharp stabs of his thick, rock hard dick prevented her from doing so.

"OMIGOD! I'M FINNIN TO CUUUMMMM!" She shreiked, giving him a seductive sneer. The one she'd perfected while dancing in strip clubs all over Philly.

"I'm about to move up in yo' spot asap! Straight up!"

He managed to say. The words almost sticking in his throat as he slammed his fuck-pole deep inside her continuously. Finally he exploded inside of her wet center.

"Mmmm... Reggo, baby, I hope you're fa-real?" She moaned happily. "Because I'd love to come home to this juicy dick every night. You wouldn't even have to work. I can take care of you, baby."

Yeah, right, he thought. *So you could rock me to sleep and have me end up like that nigga I just crushed? NO GOOD! You won't get me like that, no matter how good the pussy is.*

"I feel the same way, shawdy." Flat-Head said, full of insincerity. *Fuck you bitch! I got plans on being the next Ludacris, and watching my bank account grow to Bill Gates status. That's it. That's all! I can't do that by shacking up with your freak ass,* Flat-Head thought as she kissed him and rolled off of his limp joystick.

"Well, let's make it happen, Daddy."

"We'll work out the details when we wake up." He said, turning his back to her.

Waiting a minute...Flat grabbed his gun and closed his eyes.

Life ain't fair. And everybody, even women, were pawns in this wicked Game. The only way to survive it was to sleep with one eye open and keep your hand on the only friend that a *true go-hard* street dude could trust, Mr. Glock Forty-Nickel....

59

Chapter 17
Richly Deserved

BY THE TIME FLAT-HEAD AND FRAY RETURNED TO D.C., news of Ramel's shooting had spread across Southeast like an out of control brush-fire. The situation really pissed Flat-Head off. He felt disrespected that somebody would even fuck with someone he had genuine love for.

Flat went to see Ramel at his apartment. He walked into Ramel's room, still dazed by the shocking assassination attempt on his partner's life. He kept thinking about Ramel when they had gotten high together several days earlier -- so vibrant and alive. Now Ramel was laid back looking defeated, scared and hopeless. To Flat that didn't seem possible.

"Slim, kill my mufa', I'ma crush whoever done this shit to you." Flat muttered, feeling his face grow hot with anger. "That's straight up!"

"Why the fuck did you leave me over there in the first place?" Ramel griped, raising his voice.

He totally ignored Flat's vengeful declaration.

Ramel knew that Flat had to get ghost in a hurry. But he'd damn neared died and was hurting, so Flat had to feel his pain.

"I caught a fresh body in broad daylight, Foolio'." Flat retorted, bad-temperedly. "Fuck I s'posed to do? Just hang around until the Feds come and take me to jail?"

"Never mind. Just fuck it." Ramel sighed, taking notice of him for the first time. He sported expensive Versace gear from head to toe. *What the hell has he been doing?* Ramel wondered.

"Fuck what?" Flat raised his voice, getting animated. "Nigga, you my ace-boon-coon, and I came to see about you. I would've been came back, but I had some business outta town."

"With your new buddy in the Range?" Ramel finished his statement, adding a little sarcasm in his tone. Ramel then turned on his TV with the remote.

His moms had bought him a new 45" flat screen high definition joint to watch while he healed up -- one of the perks that came with getting shot and having a busted kneecap.

Deep down Ramel knew it was one of his mother's bribery tactics. It was to get him to stay at home, instead of venturing out into the streets. So far it was working. Yet Ramel knew that as soon as he healed up he was out of her spot.

"Yeah, I was hanging with somebody who don't cry all the time like you." Flat shot back. He wasn't too thrilled by Ramel's stank attitude.

"So that's how you feel?"

"Look Ramel, he just somebody I'm jive working to get that studio money," he explained quickly. "Slim appreciates how I saved his ass and he's been showing me love."

"That explains all that V-shit you rocking." Ramel smirked.

"Hell yeah! Ay', have you heard anything about the Feds looking for me?" Flat asked wearily, like knowing could solve the problem.

"Nah, but Mean-Gene came through and told me that some nigga who go by the name Bone was claiming you and your man's bodies and bragging about shooting me."

"Is that right?" Flat asked, frowning.

Nobody understood Flat-Head better than Ramel, not a single person in the world. And sometimes he even confused Ramel with his actions and ways. Any rational person could see that violence and revenge was on his mind right then. So Ramel tried to steer him away from that mind frame. Thinking rationally wasn't Flat's strongest suit. He wore his emotions on his sleeve and only knew how to react with violence whenever he felt violated or disrespected.

"Ay', you know I fucked that bitch, Pepa."

"Stop playing! No bullshit?" Flat asked as if surprised and then scratched his head.

"Slim, I crushed that pussy and asshole off-the-all-nighter... and guess what?"

"What?"

"The bitch is a lesbo. Her girlfriend lunched out on me and told me to stay away from Pepa." Ramel confessed, leaving out the part about the bitch trying to kill him. He wanted to holler at her personally once he healed up. Somehow Brooke had to be hunted down and paid back with extreme prejudice.

"Hold up moe," Flat spoke, invading his thoughts. He then pulled out his cellphone. "Yeah," he said shortly. "A'ight, meet me over around Southern Avenue in ten minutes... A'ight, bet!" Flat hung up, then looked at Ramel. "Ay' moe, I got some shit to handle. Do you need anything?"

"Hell yeah! I'm fucked up on the ends."

"How much you need, champ?"

"How much can you stand to donate, nigga?"

He gave Ramel an icy glare. "You just don't realize how much I fuck with you do you? Ramel, anything I got, you can get from me, slim. I don't care about none of that materialistic shit. Nor am I petty...If I got it, you can get it, simple as that." He then pulled out a huge wad of bills and tossed them onto the bed. "Don't go and spend it all in one place."

Before Ramel could say thanks or inquire about where he got all that money from, Flat turned and left the bedroom without looking back.

$ $ $

It was now time to think, plan and execute, Ramel reminded himself. He thought about Brooke's crazy ass, her attack on him and everything he'd done in life leading up to that point. As he began counting the money on the bed, Ramel felt that he hadn't done anything drastic enough for her to try to take him out. With that in mind, he knew she needed more than one lesson in retribution.

Should her immediate family die? A simple enough task to execute with the right amount of cash. *Richly deserved,* but was it the most effective lesson? Since he wasn't sure, the answer was probably no. Besides, there was another target to consider...A grudge to settle. *What could be better than that?*

Revenge is not a motive, it's an emotional response, Ramel knew, and he was so emotional right then. He re-counted the $11,758 that Flat-Head had given him again and again and again. He smiled, because it was *richly deserved.*

Chapter 18
Everything's A Test

FRAY FELT THAT D.C. was becoming the same boring and antiseptic place that every other major city had became. As capitalism and multinational businesses spread everywhere and major crime followed and spread as well.

Fray spent part of the day cruising through one of the world's most influential cities conducting illegal business. He'd gained twelve kilos of cocaine and $386,000 from his last robbery in Philly. Fray gave Flat $100,000 just to see what the wild youngster would do with the money.

Once Fray saw that Flat-Head didn't splurge wildly on dumb materialistic things, he decided to introduce Flat to some of the good dudes he'd been dealing with in the city; in an effort to pass Flat the torch. Fray was at the point in the Game where he wanted to retire, but alot of the people depended on him to eat.

"Where we going, slim?" Flat-Head asked after getting into Fray's truck.

"To get this money, nigga. I know you ain't think that was all I was gonna hit you off with?"

"On the up-and-up I jive did, slim...because it was your lick, and I know you have to eat too." Flat reasoned, surprising Fray. Yet, he too had been surprised by Fray.

Everytime I make a decision to rob this nigga, he always come at me with something "on the straight-up tip" to keep me second guessing myself about getting his ass. I guess I gotta give him another pass, Flat thought while looking out the window.

"Listen Flat, you saved my ass. For that alone I owe you my life. Anything I got you can get it at anytime, no questions asked. I just threw that hundred grand to see how you was gonna act. Always remember, *everything in life is a test* and a learning experience."

"So you was testing me, huh?"

"Straight up!" Fray giggled, mocking Flat-Head's famous one-liner before pulling out into traffic.

Even though Flat found Fray's punchline amusing, he choked back his laughter. Flat wanted to keep his guards and serious front up, because he knew that he was under Fray's ever watchful microscope.

Every move is a calculated step... To bring me closer...to accumulate the wealth... Til' there's nothing left. Flat-Head thought, watching Fray speed towards Congress Park Projects. A ten block walk away from Valley Green Projects.

After Fray sold two kilos and introduced Flat to Bucky Fields -- a stand up hustler/head bussa'. They shook hands and Fray told Bucky Fields that Flat would be taking over his empire soon.

"Moe, I'ma always fuck wit' you on the strength that you fuckin' wit' a good nigga. This my man," Bucky Fields stated while they shared a blunt full of Purple Haze and P.C.P.

"Slim is jive getting it, huh?" Flat-Head asked after Fray pulled off.

"I guess he doing his thing. All I do is keep two to three bricks ready for him every month. And he gets them up offa' me like clockwork. I let him get two for forty-thou', which is a big steal, because all bricks be going for twenty-five thou' a wop."

"Shid', it's all free money anyway. I'd let them joints go for eighteen-five a piece if I was getting niggas like you was getting them. That's straight up!"

"When it's your turn to burn, do what you feel is right. But until then, just lay back and learn from the master." Fray said and headed for the Suitland Parkway.

"You got that, slim." Flat-Head replied as Fray drove towards Eastgate Projects on the other side of Southeast.

Fray decided to go holler at Eastgate Fats. He was the guy that ran things around there. Fray had met Eastgate Fats when the two of them were going back and forth to Oakhill Juvenile detention center.

Oakhill Academy (B.K.A O-Kill) was the worst juvenile

detention center known to the youth of the District of Corruption. 0-Kill housed, raised and bred all the future ghetto stars, hustlers, robbers, killers, and scared niggas who'd now messed the game up in D.C. with all that snitching shit!

"Ay', roll something up, Flat. Straight up!" Fray urged, "The weed in the glove compartment."

"You better get the fuck outta my face with that bullshit!" Flat snapped, feeling the effects of the P.C.P. and Purple Haze mixture. "Fuck I look like, yo' flunky? On some real shit, stop playing with me, Fray. Straight up!"

"Geeking ass nigga, roll that shit up!" Fray drove, shaking his head in disgust. *Damn, this a hard nigga to deal with,* he thought.

"I'ma do the shit this time, but don't make it no mothafuckin' habit... and that's on some serious shit!" Flat-Head retorted as Fray eased off of East Capitol Street's Bridge, turned right on Benning Road, and sped towards Eastgate Housing Project.

Chapter 19
Eastgate Fats

When Fray pulled up, he saw why they were making major loot on this side of Southeast. The streets were packed with kids, hustlers, women, and fiends. It looked like one huge block party. Somewhat similar to the crowds of people flocking to Times Square in New York on New Years Eve.

The hustlers were serving everything from X-tacy pills, crack, cocaine and heroin; to marijuana, P.C.P, and hashish herbs, to the fiends out in the open like they were trading and selling merchandise at the Compton Swap Meet.

As Fray exited the Range Rover, he spotted the oyster-white hued throwback SL 600 Mercedez Benz sitting on deep dish classic chrome rims. Fray smiled, knowing that the vehicle belonged to none other than Eastgate Fats.

Big boy is still stuck in the late eighties and early nineties, Fray thought. Seeing all eyes directed towards his way, Fray adjusted his belt buckle. He felt the Glock-40 in his waistband, hoping nobody would do anything stupid enough to make him use it.

Word on the street had it that Eastgate Fats was sitting on a gold-mine and making more money than he could count. Fray wanted to talk to Fats, in hopes of dumping off a few kilos in that area of the city.

Fray had heard alot about several dudes from Eastgate Projects and Fats' lucrative operation also came up. A few months ago Fray dated a big mouth, gossip mongering broad named Kita. She lived in Simple City Housing Projects, but always hung out around Eastgate Projects -- Simple City's arch rival.

Simple City Projects sat directly across Benning Road

from Eastgate Projects. The two neighborhoods were often at odds. When crack cocaine exploded on the scene it intensified their differences to a whole nother level; and plenty of lives were lost during the violent beefs of the Crack Era.

Kita Goreman was known for giving the best fellatio on that side of the Anacostia River. Unbeknownest to many, Kita was also known by a select few for setting dudes up to get robbed, kidnapped, and killed for the money that they made in the streets. She'd done her homework on plenty of dudes in the Metropolitan area, and Fray would get all the juicy 4-1-1 from her.

Kita told Fray that Eastgate Fats became a natural *go-getter* once he got released from U.S.P Allenwood, after giving back a football jersey prison sentence on appeal. Kita revealed that a guy named Max was running things before Fats return to the hood.

One day Max was found dead in his car with two gunshot wounds to his skull. It was a month after Fats got out.

When Fats stepped up and took over the drug operations in Eastgate, everybody assumed that Fats was responsible for Max's untimely demise.

Fray was snatched out of his reverie after spotting Eastgate Fats walking towards him wearing a stylish Versace outfit that cost enough to feed a few hundred people in a small third world country.

Eastgate Fats gave Fray a mean-mug that would have made Satan a little nervous about getting on his bad side. Eastgate Fats stood around 5'7" and weighed roughly 265 pounds. He had a smooth chocolate candy bar complexion.

Even Fray had to admit that Fats was the flyest chubby dude on the strip.

"Man, hold the fuck up! Fray, I know that ain't you?" Fats smiled. "What's happening, baby? Boy, I was about to turn that Range into swiss cheese," he said, raising his shirt, revealing a rusty-grey Mac-11.

"When you start playing with me like dat, Fats?" Fray asked with a frown.

"Aw, coward-ass-nigga, ain't nuffin' change since O-Kill

days. Don't make me slide yo' strag-ass out here in front of everybody." Fats giggled, then threw up his hands, mimicking Bernard Hopkins' boxing style.

"Don't do it to me, baby." Fray laughed, knowing that that was how Fats greeted all of the genuine villans that he liked, respected and loved. "I gots yo' strag, nigga...but what's up, slim?"

"You, what brings you around here? You fucked up? What you need some help?" Eastgage Fats asked his old friend.

"Jive, but it's not in the aspect you're thinking on. I'm not on no gimme a hand-out type shit."

"Talk to me, baby. You know time is money out here."

"Can we go somewhere and rap?"

"Aw, scared-ass-nigga, ain't nobody gonna fuck with you while you're with me. I'm like the mayor around this muthafucka."

"I ain't worried about all 'lat, Fats. I'm worried about my trigger-happy-youngster, sitting over there in my truck, doing something real big to one of yo' men 'round here." Fray said, glancing towards his Range Rover. Fats followed his eyes and found a teen who couldn't have been no older than sixteen, looking like he'd just swallowed a raw onion.

"Fray, keep playing Fray. You gonna get you and yo' youngster fucked around, fa-real!"

"Coward-ass-nigga, you was 'noid as-e-muthafucka under that pressure. I just peeped it." Fray giggled.

"NIGGA, I AM PRESSURE!" Fats said, releasing a burly sigh. "I've been under pressure my whole life! Now what you want, strag-ass-nigga?"

Once Fray explained his situation to Fats about getting rid of a few kilos for a low price every month, Fats nodded his head as if he were deep in thought.

"It bet' not be no garbage, Fray, because if it is, I'ma smack all the shit outta you!" Fats said in a joking manner, but meant every word.

"You smack me, the whole City will know about it after I beat the brakes off ya' big as--"

"Don't disrespect me in public, Fray." Fats cut him off.

69

"You forcing my hand, baby. You better go 'head, I'm telling you." Fats barked with a crooked smile, all the while looking around to see who was watching him. Fats loved being the center of everyone's attention.

"A'ight big boy. So how many joints you want?"

"How many you got?"

"Fats, stop playing all the time, DAMN."

"It was worth a try...coward-ass-nigga. You lucky I gots love for you. If I didn't, you and that bighead ass nigga would be running outta Eastgate ass naked."

"C'mon slim, time is money out here. Didn't you just tell me that?"

"See, that's what I'm saying... you niggas out here wanna be me! You niggas can't be Eastgate Fats! It's only one, baby! Only one!" Fats bellowed, causing everyone to look in his direction.

"I'm gone, slim. You on some bullshit. Lemme know something when you get off, okay."

"Strag-ass-nigga, I knew you couldn't take no pressure. Gimme six bricks for a hundred-thou' and get the fuck on, nigga.... before I kill you." Fats smirked.

Fray quickly headed for his truck. When he reached the truck he stopped for a brief moment, studying Eastgate Fat's body language. After being certain that no snake shit was about to take place, Fray grabbed the kilos out of the truck.

"What's up, slim? You need me to go with you?" Flat-Head asked, pulling out his gun.

"Naw, I'm cool. Just chill and watch my back."

"I got that. Straight up!" He replied, watching Fray close the door and walk towards Fats' Mercedes Benz.

Flat smiled pleasantly, playing the game also. He was now the street hustler's apprentice. If Fray noticed that Flat-Head was wearing a mask of deceit, he sure wasn't letting on.

Nothing bothers him does it? Well, I'll have to see about that, Flat thought, feeling his tail rattle right before the strike. As he watched Fray and the fly chubby guy exchange duffel bags and one arm hugs, Flat decided to go ahead with the next phase of his plans. His eyes were open and his appetite for destruction, wealth, and super-stardom were in over-drive. Things were looking up....

Chapter 20
Only Time Will Tell

THINGS BECAME HECTIC FOR A YOUNG GO-GETTER ONCE AGAIN, and the more Ramel tried to avoid the drama, the worse it got.

The drama with his moms started again. Once he told her that he'd made up his mind about moving out, she hit the roof and cursed him out visciously.

On top of that, he had Flat-Head's crazy ass pressing him everyday to come outside and play. He would drop by without calling just so he could tease Ramel about getting shot and robbed. Flat really possessed a weird sense of humor.

Between hearing moms cursing and Flat-Head's teasing, Ramel was on the verge of going beserk or having a nervous breakdown. He was still too weak to put up with their shit, because of the lingering injuries from getting shot.

Ramel had a permanent zipper like scar on his stomach where the doctors operated and extracted several bullets from his body. He also suffered nerve damage in his left leg.

After pushing himself through intensive physical therapy over the last three months, he regained some feeling, but walked with a slick limp. It added a little swagger to his persona, yet he was no where near back to being the old Ramel.

After being laid up for nearly four and a half months, Ramel only had one more day to go before he could just leave home and do his thing. Leaving home would be the hardest thing that he'd ever had to do. Up until that point in his life when he'd gotten shot, Ramel knew how much his moms wanted to protect him from the evil that men did. However he wanted to be a rebel, which was hard for her to grasp. Ramel insisted on doing things on his own, and experiencing what the streets had to offer.

Maybe you can imagine what he was feeling at the time, or maybe nobody ever will, unless they lived through the same shit.

His independence was everything he'd ever wanted. All the sleepless nights, all the times he'd endured her merciless bullying and emotional abuse; all the life lessons and slugs he took, Ramel felt he deserve it. Now he was somewhat nervous; his stomach was tied in a sailor's knot, preparing to face the cold-hearted world again.

Legends are made in this town. One day my name could be famous too... Only time will tell, he thought.

With that bubbling on his mind, Ramel knew this was it. Tomorrow when he stepped outside to face the world, he'd either ball or fall; gunning for that one big shot everybody says they wanted. That shot so many people never got, and he sure never thought he'd get it either after getting shot.

Yet Ramel had eaten those hot balls like Scobby Snacks. He felt invincible! He felt that God had a purpose for his life. His drive to shine grew larger and unbelievably louder. His young mind began visualizing luxury cars and dining out amongst the stars. The visions carried him higher, causing an intoxication that he'd never had in life. Ramel wanted to be high like that all the time.

The feeling told him that he could succeed and be the architect of his own destiny.

He sat and allowed the feeling to get the best of him. It felt better than any dream he'd ever had. And Ramel vowed to make it happen for real -- by any means necessary....

Chapter 21
Someone's Blood

ON THE WAY HOME LATE THAT SAME NIGHT, Flat-Head was guilt tripping a little, and kind of shaky about what Ramel had told him. Still, he felt he'd had no choice. If he hadn't reacted when he did, Fray would be dead and he wouldn't be six figures richer. Flat loved Ramel like a brother and felt that he had to get revenge for him. *Simple as that.*

Other questions burned in Flat's mind. *Why that chump Bone didn't kill Ramel? Why risk not finishing the job only to have someone come back for revenge?*

Flat sure as hell doubted that it was a coincidence that his partner had gotten shot less than 24 hours after he'd killed someone. Flat figured somebody was trying to send him a message.

Looking at his G-Shock watch and seeing that it was late, Flat tried to refocus his thinking. He wanted to think on something else, but he couldn't get his mind off of what had happened. He drove his new '96 midnight-blue Bubble Caprice Classic faster than he needed to on the mostly empty streets of Southeast, knowing he had to focus on getting out of the street life -- not digging himself deeper. It didn't really work too well though, because he wanted someone's blood for the atrocity dealt to his partner.

After pulling into Linda Pollin's parking lot, Flat-Head sat in the car for a few minutes. He tried to clear his head before heading inside for the night. Focusing on things he thought, *I need to call Fray and set things up for our next caper.* Flat felt as though his head would explode soon. And he knew he'd continue to feel that way until he got revenge for Ramel.

Finally exiting his car, Flat spotted Bone creeping through the cut with a freaky hoodrat named Jamilla. Flat-Head couldn't believe the gift he'd just received from the game-god.

Ducking and sprinting past an old abandoned car sitting on bricks in the parking lot, Flat eased his handgun out quickly, all the while watching the couple. He wanted to cut them off before they reached their destination. He thought about sitting down and waiting. He quickly tossed that idea out of his mind, knowing he wouldn't be able to sleep if he allowed the perpetrator to get away.

"C'mon Jamilla. You know I don't fuck with these yammaz' around here." Bone griped as they reached her building's backdoor.

"I'm coming, boy," she whined, giving him a kiss on the lips, all the while trying to open the back door.

"BITCH MOVE!" Bone growled, pushing Jamilla out of the way of gunfire and reaching for his gun.

Flat-Head already had his gun out, firing it rapidly.

Flat shot Bone four times, once in the throat, once in the chest, and twice in the forehead. Bone died on his feet.

Flat-Head felt intoxicated after the kill, not to mention the good rest he knew was forthcoming for getting Ramel's revenge.

"AAAAHHHHHH! AAAAAHHHHH! YOU KILLED HIM! WHY! AAAHHH!" Jamilla screamed, then began shouting for help. She tried to run in the other direction.

Quite the snitch, Flat thought and went after her. He pulled the trigger with ease, catching Jamilla high in the back.

As she fell to the ground, Flat moved for her quickly. He stood over her and pulled the trigger until she stopped moving.

Running home without looking back, Flat entered the house quietly, then eased into the kitchen to grab a bite to eat. Soon as he opened the fridge he heard a noise behind him.

He spun on his heels, gun out, holding it with two hands, ready to kill again. He lowered his weapon after seeing his father standing there in the doorway. His dark-brown eyes fired up, his anger evident.

"Boy, what the fuck is your problem? I know that wasn't

you out there just shooting and shit?" He snapped.

Putting his gun away, Flat sat down at the kitchen table, then stared at his father until he sat down. His father wanted to know what was going on.

Over some cold chicken and a big glass of Kool Aid, Flat-Head told his father everything he could about what had happened to Ramel, in hopes of justifying what had led him, his son, to commit a double homicide.

"What's done is done," his father sighed in disgust. "First thing tomorrow, you're leaving town until things cool down. We'll find a way to work through this together, okay."

"But Pop--"

"POP MY ASS!" He barked, raising his voice. "I'm not letting you go to jail and be around the same shit I had to be around. It's not healthy. It's not the life for you. You tried things your way, it didn't work. From now on, you'll have to do it my way," he said, then got up and left Flat in the kitchen to ponder the seriousness of what he'd gotten himself into...

$ $ $

THE FOLLOWING MORNING, Flat-Head was awakened by his father yelling at someone in the front room.

"MUTHAFUCKA! I DONE TOLD YOU, NOT IN HERE! WHY ARE YOU FUCKING WITH US ANYWAY, WHEN BIN LADEN'S STILL ON THE LOOSE AND TRYNA KILL YOU DUMB MUTHAFUCKAS! YEAH, YOU MUTHAFUCKAS IS SCARED OF THEM MOUNTAIN, CAVE LIVING MUTHAFUCKAS, HUH?"

Jumping out of bed, Flat grabbed his gun and peeked out of his bedroom. Hearing the low sounds of walkie-talkies, Flat-Head knew that the Feds had come to arrest him.

"Shit!" He cursed under his breath and closed the door.

Damn, my father jive go hard as shit for me, Flat-Head thought while dressing quickly. Soon as he went for the window, Flat heard some scuffling and running footsteps getting louder.

76

"FREEZE MOTHERFUCKER!" A cop yelled as Flat dove out of the bedroom window.

Hitting the grass with a loud thud, Flat rolled over and jumped up running. If he would've been on point he would've peeped the cops waiting on him near his planned escape route.

Before Flat-Head could turn the corner, several cops bent the corner and tackled him as if he was a football player trying to return a kick-off.

"GET THE FUCK OFFA' ME!" Flat-Head yelled.

"No can do, killer!" Smirked Detective Freeman from the warrant division. "Your ass is grass, bub."

As the cops handcuffed Flat and took him to an awaiting police car, he lowered his head. He didn't really care about getting caught, but the charges they had on him were puzzling him. It was the only thing he could think about.

Sitting in the police car, Flat saw the police exit his house with two of his handguns sealed inside a plastic ziplock bag. Then, remembering the night before, Flat felt guilty. If the police ever found out about what he'd done, he knew his life would be over. Flat couldn't believe that he had gotten caught slipping like that.

How can I get up outta this shit? Damn, I fucked up big time. I gotsta' get up out of here before they trace one of them guns to them bodies I just caught. Damn, I fucked up big time... Just calm down and see what they got on you. If it's hectic, then I'ma have to call Fray for some assistance, he thought, seeing the detectives smile triumphantly as they held up the guns they'd found for him to see.

"You're going down, Flat-Head!" Detective Freeman mouthed to Flat-Head and slowly turned an upright thumb downward.

Seeing that, Flat-Head knew that facing the hard-nose detective and the corrupted and racist justice system would be the hardest thing he'd ever have to face alone.

Chapter 22
Hoe Problems

"Bitch, where the fuck have you been at?" Pepa hissed as soon as Brooke entered the apartment.

Since going over the edge and nearly killing Ramel over her, Brooke decided to stay away from Pepa until she got her mind right. Walking past Pepa, Brooke gave her the silent treatment.

"Brooke, I know damn well you hear me talking to you. Why you carrying me and shit?" Pepa raised her voice.

Rolling her pretty brown eyes, Brooke retorted, "If you would've never broken our bond and trust factor, I wouldn't be carrying your trifling ass."

"What's that 'pose to mean? What kind of shit is that to say?" Pepa fumed. "Bitch, we fuck niggas all the time for money. That's our hustle, or did you forget?"

"Pepa, I told your ass when we first started making love that I love hard. I remember specifically telling you don't ever betray my love! What you thought, I was playing? Why you go and fuck that nigga Ramel? On top of that, you paid him. Bitch, don't lie, because I heard ya'll whole conversation that morning before I confronted you." Brooke revealed.

"I'm not gonna be sitting up here explaining myself no more to yo' dumb ass. You is lunching!"

"Whatever, freak-ass bitch!"

"Oh, so I'ma freak now?" Pepa stated nastily.

"Did I sta-sta-stutter?"

Hearing the sarcasm dripping in her tone, Pepa remained speechless, standing there looking evilly at Brooke.

"Yeah, I don't hear yo' smart-ass mouth now. Speak up, you freak-ass bitch!" Brooke got louder, getting up in Pepa's

78

face.

"I can't stand you, bitch!" Pepa hissed.

"Then why you tripping on whether or not if I come or go? Bitch, I do as I please."

"I don't care whatchu' do, Brooke. So..." Pepa said. This time her voice cracked.

"So what? What are you tryna say, Pepa?"

"I'm saying fuck you! It's over!"

Face to face, they stared at each other until several tears fell from Brooke's eyes.

"IT'S NEVER OVER!" Brooke yelled, raising her fists.

Pepa jumped back as Brooke charged at her. Brooke backed her up against the wall and began punching her in the face.

"BITCH, I'MA KILL YOUR ASS! AAAHHHH!" Pepa wailed and began scratching and pulling out Brooke's hair.

"Pepa, stop it bitch...AAHHH!" Brooke laughed, squeezing Pepa in a bear hug and burying her head in Pepa's neck until she calmed down.

"That shit is not funny, Brooke. Get the fuck offa' me, now! You need to stop playing with me!"

"You're the one around here fucking niggas behind my back, and paying them for the dick. That shit hurts real bad, Pep'."

"Look, I'm sorry. That shit I did with Ramel was nothing. I was just weak and horny. I don't want to be with nobody but you. That's fa-real." Pepa confessed.

"Prove it, then." Brooke said, grabbing Pepa's tiny waist and pushing her back up against the wall.

When Pepa kissed her, Brooke began crying. She knew that she wasn't ever giving up on Pepa's love. She just wanted to make her suffer a little bit. Even though they fucked and sucked men for the love of money, Brooke loved Pepa unconditionally, and she was not about to let her go. Pepa had cheated and made her nearly kill. Brooke felt like a fool, but she didn't care.

All she wanted was her girlfriend. Nobody had ever

79

made her feel the way that Pepa did. Brooke was crazy in love. The more they kissed, the more they got turned on and wet.

"I love you, Brooke."

"I said, prove it slut." She whispered, sucking on her neck.

Making her way down, Pepa raised Brooke's summer dress and then took her thong off. Holding onto her head, Brooke lifted one leg over Pepa's shoulder so that Pepa's tongue could find its way to her dripping hot love-oven.

"Mmmmmmm... I missed you sooo much." Pepa moaned, shaking her tongue gently along Brooke's pulsating slit.

Pepa's tongue gently licked in and out of Brooke's pussy and around her clit, causing Brooke to cry out in ecstasy. She tried to fight the feelings of pleasure, but the combination of Pepa's tongue and her fingers probing her asshole had her on cloud-99. The next thing Brooke knew, she found herself lying on the floor in a 69 position, sucking on Pepa's juicy pussy. They sucked and pleasured one another until both climaxed on each other's tongues....

Chapter 23
Trouble Ahead

A MONTH AND A HALF LATER, Ramel found himself hanging out with Flat-Head's partner, Fray, on a daily basis. If he wasn't with him, he would either be fucking Pepa, or somewhere scheming on another unsuspecting female's riches.

After learning about Flat-Head's arrest, Ramel got worried immediately. Also the hood had begun to talk about the murders of the guy Bone, who robbed him, and that hoodrat, Jamilla. When Ramel heard that they were implicating Flat as the killer, he told him to go find the best criminal defense lawyer in The District.

After a little hesitation, Flat finally hired Jennifer Hicks. At that time she was the best defense attorney in the city. On top of his finding her, Flat-Head began having sex with her on a few of his legal visits. He was supposed to be trying to get out, yet he was humping his attorney! That's Flat-Head for you.

Jennifer did eventually help Flat beat the two murder-one charges at his month long-trial. Flat-Head still had to do ten months down Oakhill juvenile facility for being convicted for the guns they found in his house.

Scared wasn't the word to describe how Ramel felt after Flat revealed that he'd taken care of his light work for him. Flat sat on a social visit with Fray, some broad he knew, and Ramel, acting like he didn't have a care in the world. When the girl and Fray excused themselves to get some refreshments, Flat dropped that bomb on him. There weren't many dudes in the city who were willing to kill for a friend, but Flat-Head was one of them. Ramel didn't know what he was going to do to repay him. Getting blood on his hands wasn't in the cards for him. It had never even crossed his mind. Ramel never thought that just mentioning a person's nickname who'd done something to him could lead to that person's death; and him visiting and sending Flat money every weekend. It's a good thing that he hadn't mentioned Pepa's girlfriend, Brooke, because she would've got whacked too.

Ramel knew right off the bat that Flat-Head would want him to get wicked with them pistols like him, which was a problem. Ramel just didn't know if he wanted that kind of lifestyle, because he wasn't prepared to become some graveyard's fertilizer. Plus there was the fact that he didn't need to. He knew how to scam and con women on the streets. And he was getting better with each passing day. This hustle helped him to see all of the games and angles that women played, which would ultimately help him see any game coming in his direction.

On the other hand, with Flat-Head's hustle, he would be blind as a bat trying to see the drama coming -- which was death play. Flat-Head made so many enemies that he had to look over his shoulder every time he moved. Ramel didn't want to live like that.

"Slim, I got eight more months, then I touch down." Flat-Head said, invading Ramel's thoughts. Flat immediately began making plans for the two of them to move into a house together.

Ramel wanted nothing more than to chill with Flat-Head and make some money. Because despite his flaws and wild ways, Flat was a real go-getter. Still, Ramel wasn't feeling the move.

"Look Flat, I appreciate what you did for me, but I'm...I'm just not with all that wild shit you be doing."

"WHAT THE FUCK YOU MEAN YOU NOT WITH IT!" Flat-Head yelled, causing people to stare in their direction. "NIGGA, I'M IN THIS MOTHAFUCKA, CAUSE I FUCKS WITH YOU! STRAIGHT UP!"

"I'm just saying, I'm into working them broads. I don't know if I'm ready to kill somebody. That ain't me. Some niggas are killers, some are hustlers, some are pimps... different strokes for different folks. I want to do other shit with my life." Ramel spoke, looking down at his fresh beef and broccoli hued Timberlands. He would never admit it, but he felt intimidated by Flat.

"You can still work the bitches and do whatever you wanna do, but you're not turning your back on me, ever...Especially not after what I did for you." Flat scolded Ramel like he was a child.

"So you gonna throw that shit in my face? I never told you to do that shit. You did that cause you wanted to."

"Naw, I did it cause I had to. I fucks with you, and there's a lot that comes with that, even putting in work."

"I hear you." Ramel mumbled.

"Don't play with me, Ramel. I'm crushing shit. Don't be my next vic'! Straight up!"

"Fuck you, Flat." Ramel playfully said, wondering if Flat-Head really meant what he'd just said.

"That's the nigga I know." Flat smirked, hugging Ramel.

Barely hugging him back, Ramel recognized just how much Flat fucked with him. He tried to avoid the conversation, for Ramel knew that Flat would pull the *I'm locked up for you* card, and he would give in. Ramel had to get Flat-Head's back, because he had his. Flat had Ramel by the balls and he hated every minute of it.

"Ay' Fray, look out for my man, and get him all the bitches he wants. Straight up!" Flat-Head spoke through a crooked smile.

"I gotchu', slim. Everything is gonna be proper by the time you come home."

"It better be, or it's gonna be a killing on the first night! Straight up!" Flat said, glancing sideways at Ramel.

While Fray, Flat and the girl laughed and talked for the rest of the visit, Ramel's head began spinning, because be knew deep down inside that hanging with Flat-Head, there would be nothing but trouble ahead.

$ $ $

83

AFTER LEAVING THE SOCIAL VISIT WITH FLAT, Fray and Ramel dropped Flat's girlfriend off and changed clothes. They put on all black jeans and matching hooded sweatshirts.

The time had finally arrived to pay Brooke a long overdue visit, and Ramel needed Fray's crazy-ass for the occasion. After parking Fray's truck a few blocks away from Valley Green Projects, they walked to Pepa's building.

Going to visit Flat-Head with his girlfriend was just the diversion that Ramel needed to create an alibi for the mission he intended on carrying out.

Nobody could argue with the fact that he was in one place with several eye-witnesses, verifying his whereabouts, while something tragic went down at Brooke's crib.

Ramel knew that if he gave Flat-Head some flack about his plans, he would easily go berserk, creating a loud enough disturbance to focus all eyes on them. With that done, they only had thirty minutes to accomplish their mission before all visiting ceased at Oakhill.

"Just do everything like I told you, Fray. Don't go away from the plan."

"Young nigga, you're rolling with the master of this shit. We in and out in ten minutes." Fray retorted with a tight-face.

Flat-Head had told Ramel that Fray was always that way when it was time for drama. He believed in doing whatever job to perfection.

As the two made their way towards Pepa's front door, Fray and Ramel put on ski masks to conceal their identities.

Ramel had learned how to play on Pepa's emotions through sex, lies and more sex. He had her to the point where she was always calling him and begging for more. Pepa was ready and willing to run through Hell with gasoline thongs on, just to spend a little extra time with him. So when Ramel called her before they left Fray's crib and told her to be buck-naked and ready to fuck, she jumped at the opportunity to see him.

"Ramel, I'ma get rid of Brooke real quick, then..."

"Naw, don't do that." Ramel had cut her off. "Just leave the front door open and go into the bathroom and wait for me. I'm tryna fuck you while she's sleeping in the bedroom."

"Uh, boy, you're so nasty." She giggled, then grew silent for a minute, as if she had to think over his proposition.

"Okay Ramel, just hurry up before I change my mind. I love you, Ramel."

"I know you do." Ramel said, then hung up.

$ $ $

When he turned Pepa's doorknob, the door opened just as he expected it would. Once inside the house, Ramel and Fray made their way to the bedroom. Seeing the bathroom door closed, Ramel knew Pepa was following his orders to the tee, which made him feel proud of her and his womanizing skills.

When Ramel cracked open the bedroom door, he wasn't prepared for the sight before him. Brooke laid on her back sound asleep, buck-naked and appearing to be at peace. She apparently was a hard sleeper, because she didn't move a muscle after the two men invaded the room.

Fray gently eased his gun into her neatly shaven pussy and began pushing it in and out until she began humping back.

"MMmmmm...Baby, it's cold, but that shit feels sooo good. Put it in deeper." Brooke moaned, arching her back to meet Fray's weapon's constant pumping. She never opened her eyes.

After a moment of watching Fray do his thing, looking like he was enjoying it, Ramel tapped the freaky-ass bitch on the forehead. Her eyes fluttered open. Her expression quickly showed fear.

"Surprise bitch!" Ramel growled between clenched teeth, then pulled off his mask so she could see his face. "You see what happens when you get caught sleeping." Brooke jumped and almost made Fray shoot her. Ramel just stared at her like she'd gotten caught with her hand in the cookie jar.

Brooke nearly defecated on herself. She couldn't say a word. She was in a very compromising position. She knew her life was in his hands and she hated it. Fray quickly put her in a choke-hold and began slapping his cunt-juice coated pistol in her face and mouth.

Where is Pepa? I hope they haven't killed her? What is he

going to do to me? I knew I should've killed him when I had the chance. Brooke thought, assuming her fate was about to be sealed, because of the mistakes she had made in the past.

"You see how easy it is for me to kill you? Get your freak-ass up... Oh, don't even think about putting on any clothes. You won't need none for where you're going." Ramel said as Fray yanked her out of bed roughly.

Before Brooke could scream, Fray slapped a wad of duct tape over her mouth and tied her arms and ankles together; then carried her into the front room. She tried to resist, but Fray manhandled her like she were a rag doll.

"Bitch, if you even think about making any moves or noises when we get in the hallway, I'ma make it very painful for you to breathe." Ramel threatened.

He then ran back into the bathroom and gave Pepa the quickie he'd promised her. She got so excited that she gave him a shot of her tight asshole as an added bonus for him coming to see her on such short notice.

"When are you coming to see me again?" She asked, stepping into the hot bath water she'd just ran.

She's trying to mess with my head. She thinks giving me some anal will give her power over me? It almost did! Ramel thought. But her questioning his return brought him back to his senses.

"Pepa, you know I don't roll on your time, so we're not going to start nothing new. But since you're cool with me, I'm not gonna get mad about your line of questioning. Matter of fact, when you get that money right for me, that's when I'll be back." Ramel said, mimicking Arnold Schwarzenegger's famous line from the Terminator film.

Looking at her shocked expression, he erupted with laughter, then left the bathroom. Before Pepa could say a word, Ramel was out of the apartment and on his way to finish up the job on Brooke....

Chapter 24
Temperature Check

AT THE SAME TIME Flat-Head was exiting his cell, Big Bug and Lil Greg, two thugs from Wellington Park, approached him. Big Bug stood around 6'1", weighed roughly 245 pounds, all chubbiness -- no muscles. Lil Greg was a lighter, shorter and skinnier version of the chubby brown-skin killer.

Big Bug and Lil Greg had grown up fast and rough on the streets of D.C. They were close like brothers and had five other thugs in their mob that were cold blooded killers. Big Bug always talked too much shit, of course he would back it up when it came to blows, knife play or gun play. The man just loved drama. On the flip-side, Lil Greg (A.K.A. D.C.) was mostly quiet. He only spoke with his guns and knives, which was why he received so much love from his peers around Wellington Park. Lil Greg was an animal when it came to violence. He always stayed ready to ride or die for his hood and friends.

"Ay' moe, kill my mufa', it's some lame niggas in the day room saying that your man Fray is hot."

"Stop playing, Bug.   Straight up!" Flat-Head snapped, getting angry.

"Slim, he ain't bullshitting." Lil Greg added, which made Flat take the accusations serious, because he knew that Lil Greg never went around starting trouble like Big Bug.

"D.C., do you still got that pole joint?" Flat asked.

Without answering, Lil Greg passed Flat the shiv and stepped back.

"Watchu' 'bout to do with that, moe?" Big Bug asked, giggling. He lived for drama and couldn't function right if there wasn't any chaos going on around him.

"I'm finna go check these nigga's temperature. Straight up!" Flat-Head said, concealing the shiv and heading for the TV room with Big Bug and Lil Greg on his heels...

Chapter 25
Ramel's Mercy

SOMEWHERE IN AN ABANDONED ROW HOUSE IN SOUTHEAST, Ramel took the duct tape from Brooke's mouth and smiled. His plan involved Fray playing the bad guy, he'd rough her up a little, then Ramel would step in as her savior. That way, he figured she'd always be in debt to him for sparing her life.

"You see, I want to let you live, but my man here wants to kill you for what you done to me at the hospital. All I wanna know is why did you try to kill me?" Ramel asked, watching Fray place a gun to her temple.

"Ramel, I'm sooo sorry! Please forgive me...I was tripping over my girl, Pepa. Please don't kill me." She pleaded and started crying.

"Gimme one good reason why I should let you live?"

"Because I know a whole rack of niggas in this city that's getting money. I can set them up for you, if you want."

"That's not good enough, bitch! You can do the same thing to me when you get ready." Ramel said and Fray pulled the trigger. Brooke squeezed her eyes shut and prepared for death. When she heard metal clicking against metal, she pissed in the leather wing-back chair, then slowly opened her eyes. Ramel's crooked smirk was there to greet her.

"Brooke, I can either give or take your life when you least expect it. I'm God to you now, and I'm giving you my mercy. This mercy comes with a price. Do you want my mercy?"

Brooke heard Fray cock back his weapon at the conclusion of Ramel's question. She didn't want to find out if the gun would work or not the second time around. With fear consuming her body, Brooke blurted an answer quickly, hoping it would save her life. She would worry about revenge later.

"Yes...Yes, Ramel, I want your mercy. Thank you for sparing me! I promise I'll always do whatever you want." *At least until I find a way to get your ass back, and destroy you for your actions committed against me today,* she thought, looking at him.

"I'ma hold you to that, Brooke. Oh, before you go, you can start repaying me by giving my partner and me some head." Ramel said as Fray untied her.

Ramel knew that he was going out on a limb by letting her live, but he figured she could be a future asset in helping his bank account grow bigger.

OOOOHHH! I swear to God I'ma get both of these mothafuckas back. If it takes the last breath in my body, these bastards will pay with their lives, Brooke told herself while easing out of the chair.

Without fussing, Brooke walked over to Ramel's chair and stood in front of him. Fray sat down as she leaned her Hershey chocolate colored behind ever so he could see it jiggle when she squatted rapidly.

"You promise you won't kill me?" She asked timidly, all the while pulling Ramel's dick free from his sweats.

"We're bonded for life, Brooke. You went at me, and I came at you. Now that we've settle our differences, we can move on as a team. Simple as that. Ain't no hard feelings." Ramel ended smoothly.

BULLSHIT! THERE WILL ALWAYS BE HARD FEELING UNTIL I GET YOUR ASS, Brooke said to herself. "I hope it ain't," Brooke lied with a crooked smile.

She then got down on all fours and deepthroated Ramel like she was that bitch Superhead, Karrin Stephens. Brooke made those loud slurping sounds whenever her mouth bobbed up and down on Ramel's dick. It was some straight pornographic type shit.

She was so loud and into her performance that she excited Fray. He stood up, dropped his pants and eased behind her, all the while fondling his man-meat.

"AAAAHHHHHH! NO, BOY... Na-na-not back there!" She shrieked as Fray penetrated her bunghole from the back.

"Shut up, bitch, befoe' I kill yo' ass!" Fray growled, grabbing her hair roughly and drilling in and out or her torrid milkyway like a *porno-actor* auditioning for his first anal film, trying to break into the industry.

Brooke continued begging for him to stop drilling her forbidden fruit, which only intensified Fray's pleasure. Ignoring her, Fray fucked her harder and faster, causing her lips to tighten up, putting more suction pressure on Ramel's dick. Before Ramel knew it, Brooke began screaming in ecstasy while Fray butt-fucked her. When he was ready to explode, Ramel extracted his tubesteak and squirted semen all over her face.

Fray exploded a little while later, laughing as he pulled out of her gaping anus.

"Ay' Brooke, don't forget that you owe me big time." Ramel said, looking at her curled up into a fetal position and shaking like she was having a seizure.

"Mmmm-Hmmm... I hear you." She mumbled as Ramel dropped a $20 bill and some clothes on the floor for her.

Once he was sure that she was okay, him and Fray left the row house to hit the streets and add another chapter to their uncertain futures....

Chapter 26
Who's The Real Enemy?

IT DIDN'T TAKE LONG FOR Flat-Head to step to the dude that was spreading salt on his crime partner's name. After hearing the guy out, Flat-Head's anger had reached it's peak, and he wanted blood behind the bogus accusations.

"That's a true bill, slim. I ain't got no reason to salt your man down. Respect the game, that nigger's fucked up, slim... He's hot! He told on my uncle back in the day. He got my uncle seventy six-to-life." Lovy said with a wicked sneer.

Leo "Lovy" Mathis was another young hustler from the Trinidad section of Northeast who rolled with some helluva dudes from Montello Avenue. Lovy's family was heavy in the drug game in that area. They were quick to punish anybody with swift violence. And that went for anyone that got out of line or messed with one of their folks.

Young and dumb, Flat let his mind play tricks on him. He never took a minute to investigate the accusations. He took the truth for a lie, figuring the boy was trying to get a rep' on Fray's good name. With that in mind, Flat labeled Lovy as an enemy.

"Bitch ass nigger, where's the paperwork to back up yo' story?" Flat-Head hissed, causing all eyes to focus on him.

"WHAT!" Lovy barked, catching an attitude. "Nigga, I was..."

Before he could finish, Flat-Head whipped out the shiv and stabbed Lovy in the face and chest. Flat-Head just missed severing Lovy's jugular vein as Lovy made several moves and pushing efforts to get away. As Lovy ran for safety, Flat was right on his heels, stabbing him in the back. Lovy turned around to fight him off.

"BREAK IT UP NOW! MOVE! MOVE! MOVE!" Several

counselors screamed continuosly, while rushing over to restrain Flat.

"I bet yo' bitch ass won't open your mouth again 'bout shit you don't know about!" Flat snarled and kept talking shit as the counselors escorted him to solitary confinement.

Once the iron cell door closed, Flat laid back on the thin mattress and began thinking. He tried to figure out who was his real enemy, Lovy? Big Bug? Lil Greg or Fray?

Committed to going hard, Flat really didn't give a fuck about the outcome of his actions that day. All Flat-Head knew was that he wanted to be on top, and he was more than willing to do whatever was necessary to get there.

What Flat-Head didn't know was that Lovy suffered several deep stab wounds. His left eye was permanently damaged after getting punished for blabbing his mouth.

Standing at 5'5" and weighing 145 pounds, Lovy knew he was too small to tangle with the more aggressive and stronger thug. Now, fighting for his life and licking his wounds, Lovy realized that he never stood a chance.

Now he wanted payback.

Soon as Lovy got patched up at the hospital, he called his folks and let them know everything that happened to him. From accussing Fray, all the way up to the assault that Flat-Head had did to him over a snitch.

"I want that muthafucka six feet deep! He got to go for what he did to me." Lovy cried over the phone to one of his uncles.

After ordering an assassination on Flat-Head, Lovy's uncle assured him that his wishes would be granted...

Chapter 27
Damn Fats?!

FRAY HAD JUST UNLOCKED THE DOOR of his brand new Yukon Denali XL, it was parked a block away from The Shrimp Boat seafood restaurant on East Capitol Street. When out of nowhere a dark late model Cadillac Sedan pulled up alongside Fray. He swung fast, whipping a gun from his belt.

"Get the fuck in, now," Eastgate Fats said from the driver's seat. "I said now, coward-ass nigga!"

Re-locking his SUV, Fray slid into the Cadillac. Eastgate Fats sped off as soon as Fray had closed the door. Fats kept switching lanes and checking the rearview mirrors repeatedly as if someone was following him.

Fray always remembered Fats as being someone who always stayed in an upbeat mood; always with a crooked smile.

But Eastgate Fats wasn't smiling today.

"Fuck is wrong witchu', nigga?" Fats demanded. His chubby forearms flexed against the steering wheel, the muscles of his face stiffened to the point that his mouth barely seemed to move when he spoke.

"Fats, I don't know what the fuck you're talking about!"

"If you don't it's gonna be a serious misunderstanding, Fray. I kill niggas for less than whatchu' carried me for. What's up with that muthafuckin' garbage you sold me?"

"This shit is about that *yack'* I sold you?" Fray realized.

Eastgate Fats' eyes blazed at Fray from the diver's seat. "You muthafuckin' right it's about that bullshit you sold me. And you or somebody gonna pay me back for the loss I took."

"Hold up, Fats. Whatchu' tryna --"

"HOLD UP, SHIT!" Fats raised his voice. "Nigga, you sold me a rack of Pro-Cane, and you gotsta reimburse me. Simple as that. I tried to do your coward-ass a favor and you tried to work me... Ha-Ha...You almost got away though. You had the right idea, but the wrong muthafuckin' gangsta."

Something heavy sank into Fray's stomach after hearing Fats' revelation about the drugs he brought back from Philly.

"C'mon, Fray. I don't have time to be bullshittin' about my cake. Now, what's up?"

Fray didn't say a word, but Fats continued griping away. "I put that garbage-ass shit out on the block and ended up losing all my clientele to them Simple City niggas. Do you know what the fuck that means?"

When Fray didn't answer, Fats screeched around the corner, eyes still darting back and forth from the rearview mirror to Fray. "Don't get fucked around about this shit, Fray. You can't go 'round beating muthafuckas. Especially not me! Matter of fact, how in the fuck did your coward-ass even get the heart to try me?"

"Ay' Fats..."

"Fats, shit. GET MY MONEY, NIGGA!"

"Stop the car, Fats."

"Aw' coward-ass nigga--"

"LET ME OUT, NOW!" Fray bellowed, pulling out his gun.

Eastgate Fats screeched to a halt on a side street running up a hill, pinning Fray's door too close to a parked car, stopping him from opening the door.

"Fray, don't make me fuck you up." Fats barked. "Nigga, you just pulled a gun on me?"

"Fats, I don't be on joke time all the time. Just pull up and let me out. I'ma get your cake back to you in a few days."

Fats didn't move.

"It didn't take you a few days to take my shit! Fray, my patience is wearing real thin with you. I usually kill niggas for less than the shit you pulled on me."

Fray slammed open the door and tried to squeeze himself through. Fats lunged over and grabbed Fray's arm, the one holding the gun. Fray latched a hand onto Fats' wrist and yanked away, simultaneously pulling the trigger accidentally.

"BOOM!" the gun exploded.

Fats grunted in agony and pulled his hand away. Looking down, he covered his bleeding stomach where Fray had just shot him.

Fray smashed the window with his gun, shattering it.

"Fats, on everything, it was an accident. I swear I didn't mean to shoot you. You know you ain't s'posed to grab me like that while I got my hammer."

Fats cradled his bleeding gut. "That's the problem! You niggas think I don't s'posed to do a rack of shit. Ha-Ha..." Fats barked with a sinister smirk, then began reaching under his seat.

Fray quickly hit the window again with his elbow. The glass broke away along the fracture line left by his first strike.

"Fats, don't make this lil' episode more than it has to be. I said it was an accident." Fray explained, all the while easing himself out backwards through the window, knocking the remnants of glass aside just as Fats got his hands onto his pistol.

"BITCH-ASS-NIGGA, I'MA KILL YOU!" Fats yelled and squeezed off two rounds just as Fray's foot vanished from the car.

Fats started to get out and pursue Fray with hopes of giving him a dirt nap, but when he looked back Fray was ducking and bending the corner like an escaped convict, then Fray disappeared....

Chapter 28
Red or Green Pill?

D.C. MAY BE A CITY THAT NEVER SLEEPS, but at 4 o'clock in the morning there were parts that definitely weren't awake. One such place was the dimly lit basement of a parking garage in a scary section of Southeast. Buried three stories beneath the street, it was the perfect picture of stillness. A concrete cocoon. The only noise to be heard was the numbing buzz of the florescent lighting overhead.

That and Ramel's impatient middle finger tapping repeatedly on the steering wheel inside Flat-Head's idling bubble shaped Chevy Caprice. He was wondering where in the hell Brooke was and why did she keep standing him up.

Ramel glanced at his watch and shook his head. His finger tapping continued. Brooke was late.

Two days late, actually.

A missed appointment.

Trouble brewing? No doubt about it. She didn't seem to take Ramel serious at all. Twenty minutes later a pair of headlights finally lit up the far wall by the ramp to the next level. A white Chevy Suburban SUV appeared.

What the fuck is she doing with a big-ass truck? Ramel thought, watching the SUV slowly approach him. It stopped twenty feet away.

The engine died and Brooke stepped out. She sported some white Prada sneakers and a warm grey track suit that hugged her thick curves.

Brooke began walking towards Ramel's car. There was somebody else in her truck, but he couldn't tell if it was a man or a woman. They stayed inside. Ramel figured it had to be another female, no man in their right mind would ride

97

with a female to a secluded parking garage to meet another man, especially at 4 a.m.

Ramel got out and met her halfway.

"You must don't take me serious at all, huh?"

"Ramel, I'm sorry, but this bitch Pepa is on my back all day and night. She won't let me out of her sight." She whined and Ramel could see Pepa eyeing him with daggers in her eyes.

"That's her in the truck?"

"Yeah, she's mad. But she'll be fine. She's on me all day and night, just like you." Brooke smarted off.

"So you getting smart?"

"No," she muttered, lowering her head.

Ramel reached into his pocket and pulled out a picture, offering it to her. She studied it and gave him a confused expression.

"What's this?"

"Something I need you to handle," he started, "You know, do your thing. Once you butter up the meal, call me and I'ma stick a fork in him."

Brooke smiled and folded her arms together across her chest.

"I think I can do that for you. But after I do this we're even, right?"

Hell No! Bitch, you owe me for life. You just don't know it yet. You lucky I don't kill your ass for what you tried to do to me! Ramel thought with a smile.

"You drive a hard bargain, girl. If you pull this off, we're even." He lied. "I got something for you in the trunk."

"What?"

"Come find out."

They walked to the back of the Caprice. Ramel popped the trunk, removed a blue gym bag and placed it on the ground. Brooke looked it over for a moment.

"It's ten thousand in there. There's more where this came from if you fuck with me after this move, but it's up to you. You can take this loot now and we're even after you take care of my business. Or you can take half now, and make ten times that ten thousand in the bag by fucking with me. What's up?"

"Am I supposed to move whenever you say jump?"

Hell yeah, bitch! Ramel thought but simply said, "Of course not. I'm on your time, boo," Ramel lied. "I just wanna see you get some money for all the bullshit I put you through. Just call it a lil' payback."

Brooke grabbed the bag. "So what now?" She asked, all the while taking $5,000 out of the bag. She counted it twice, then gave it to Ramel.

"Now you get ghost." Ramel smiled, knowing her greed would keep her around for as long as he had the cash to feed her appetite. "You know you got a helluva gig to accomplish for me, right?"

"Boy, that's nothing. I'ma handle that for you. Why is this dude so special?"

"Just do good on this for me and leave it at that."

"Okay, boss."

"Don't play with me, Brooke." Ramel warned, giving her a serious look.

"Okay," she whined timidly, getting the message. They hugged and Ramel watched Pepa run a finger across her throat, threatening him with bodily harm. He knew that she was messed up behind seeing him with her lover like that. *She'll get over it once I explain things to her*, Ramel hoped.

"Tell Pepa you're hustling for me, okay. You know, to save all the drama from escalating."

"Why? You still fucking her?" Brooke grumbled.

"Just do what the fuck I say and leave it at that."

"Whatever," she hissed and walked away.

Ramel watched as Brooke carried the bag back to the SUV with an apparent attitude. The way she slammed the door and drove off, he knew her aggression was directed towards him, *but fuck it, red or green pill, you live and you learn...*

He wondered if Pepa and Brooke would be able to figure out that he intended to fuck them and use them until he got tired. Any which way, he was definitely about to get blood on his hands.

Even if he wished to hell that he wasn't, the beef with Fray

99

and Fastgate Fats was inevitable. Which brought in Flat-Head and ultimately forced him into the drama also....

Chapter 29
The Ugly Truth...

FLAT-HEAD WAS GOING STIR-CRAZY! His release date had been revoked twice by his sentencing judge due to his combative, assaultive and disobedient behavior during his stay at Oakhill Juvenile Detention Facility.

Now Flat-Head was returning to court with a 90 day good conduct report from his counselors and the warden of Oakhill. While wishing for the days to pass quickly, Flat-Head worked-out consistently and stayed to himself. Whenever he wasn't intoxicated on jail house wine and smuggled-in-weed, he would read, write his rap songs and sleep.

Hearing about the beef that Fray had gotten mixed up in with Eastgate Fats from Ramel during a visit had really changed his motivation to get back to the streets. Flat had spoken to numerous counselors and teachers and even did extra clean up duties in an effort to stunt like the model inmate that they had wanted him to be.

"Mr. Belle," the judge began in a stern tone. Flat-Head stood up and stared at the old looking white man who resembled the actor Sean Connery. "I see your dramatic turn for the better here in these reports. What brought about the sudden and drastic change?"

I need to get to the bricks and punish these niggas before they punish my man, Flat-Head wanted to say, but simply nodded his head and said, "Honestly, your Honor, I just woke up one day and decided that jail isn't the place for me. And I don't want to fuc-. I mean, I don't want to mess up my life anymore."

"I see. That's the most thoughtout articulated hogwash I've heard in *years.*" The judge said, then began wading through

101

the records and data that had been collected by the Oakhill staff for the hearing.

The judge was trying to get Flat-Head agitated and it almost worked. However, Flat-Head saw the bigger picture. Fray needed him to survive.

"Mr. Belle, if I let you go home, what are your plans?"

To kill every nigga that gets in me and my mans business, he thought but instead he said, "I'm going back to school and graduate. Then I intend to get a job in the music business."

"I'm sorry to hear about your last goal." The judge said, and although he didn't laugh, there was nothing but derision in his tone. Flat-Head wanted to kill the cracka judge for talking down on him. "But then of course, who am I to judge? I know I'm making a terrible mistake, but considering your drastic change for the better and the outstanding recommendations you've received from your counselors, I'm going to release you from The District's custody and back into the custody of your father. But I'm warning you, Mr. Belle, if you ever step foot in my courtroom again, you will regret it. Case dismissed." The judge said, banging his gavel all the while looking Flat-Head in the eyes as the Federal Marshalls escorted him from the courtroom.

Flat doubted very seriously that he would ever return to a prison cell. An idea struck him and it was hard to handle.

I am what white America wants to destroy ain't I? I am the ugly truth of Urban America....

If Flat wasn't so caught up in his thoughts, he would have noticed his father and the three pairs of eyes watching his every move as he exited the courtroom.

The same pairs of eyes that were patiently waiting on his return to the streets...so they could bury him.

Chapter 30
Get Him Girl

THE FOLLOWING AFTERNOON, Eastgate Fats walked out of his concrete kingdom in Southeast and popped opened the trunk of his big body Mercedes Benz. It was parked on Benning Road. In went his Mac-90 assault rifle and Street Sweeper Shotgun.

Taking a non-life threatening slug to the gut in the previous incident with Fray had left Fats' ego bruised, which promised nothing but beef between them. Fats knew he wouldn't rest peacefully until all of his beefs were dead and gone.

Fats pressed the button on his keyless remote and watched his surroundings as the chirps of the car alarm deactivated. That's when she caught his eye.

Got dayyum'! Fats thought, watching the woman standing in the parking lot of the Farmer's Market. She stared back at him like she wanted to eat him alive.

What is she doing around here this early in the morning? He asked himself. *Only one sure way to find out,* Fats told himself and walked straight across Benning Road to her. Fats thought she looked so friendly and sexy wearing a form fitting Prada track suit that seemed to have been painted on her curvaceous frame.

Fats felt a little suspicious, because she kept watching him from the parking lot. Or worse, paranoid. Which is why he cautioned himself not to overreact.

Seeing her assignment come her way, Brooke promptly stepped away from her car. She walked toward him seductively, giving him a friendly wave.

They met halfway.

Fats tilted his head and smiled. "If I ain't know better, I'd say you is watching me?"

"I'm guilty, Fats." Brooke smiled back after confessing that she knew his name, which caused Fats' smile to quickly turn into a stone cold frown. "But it's not whatchu' think or what it looks like. I'ma be straight up with you Fats. You can blame Fray and Ramel for this meeting we're having right now."

"Blame them for what?" Fats asked sternly, placing his hand on his 40 caliber semi-automatic.

Brooke gave Fats a blank look. "For sickin' me on you...You got some type of beef with them don't you?"

"Jive, but it ain't nothing serious." Fats lied.

"It has to be, because they want me to set you up so they can kill you." She threw that out there hoping to get his attention.

Little did she know she was telling the truth.

"They even gave me ten thousand to do this shit. Half now and the other half after they deal with you."

Fats nodded. He figured either she was telling the truth or she was a born liar. "What's your name, shawdy?"

"Brooke, I'm from The Valley, and I want to get back at them niggas, because they raped me."

"I'm saying, what does that hafta' do with me?" Fats probed, looking over his shoulder every three seconds at his car parked across the street.

"Just like they sent me atchu, they can send another bitch atchu to set you up. I can help you get them niggas out of the way for good." She looked at her watch like she had somewhere to be.

Brooke fell silent. She knew that she had captured his attention. A smug look veiled her small round face.

It's known in the streets that pussy is a nigga's quickest downfall... and it would've been mines if she would've never came clean with me. Them niggas should've never tried to get at me this way. I'ma crush them niggas, Fats thought and gave Brooke a hug.

"You know what shawdy? I digs your style. Ain't no lying in you, so I'ma fuck with you on this one here."

"I really appreciate it Fats...'cause I want some payback bad as shit on them bitch-ass niggas."

"If you play your part to the tee, you'll get it. If you fuck up or try to cross me, I'ma kill you and your whole family." Fats warned.

"I can live with that," she said meekly.

They shook hands and Brooke started to walk away.

"Oh, you know what?" She paused. "It just dawned on me that I don't have your number. You should probably gemme it."

Fats hesitated for a split second. Giving out his number was one of the last things that he wanted to do. Fats also didn't want to appear suspicious of Brooke since she came at him on a real level.

"You got that." Fats smiled. "Just remember what I just told you. You cross me, you die...You got a pen on you?"

Chapter 31
Switching Sides

Brooke called Ramel right after her meeting with Fats. She felt her initial encounter with Fats merited a report back to the person who'd threatened her life. Just in case he was following her Brooke wanted to rock Ramel all the way to sleep, then reveal her ugly head in hopes of seeing him die for the violation he committed against her.

"Did he suspect anything crudely from you?"

"That's what you want to know first?"

"Hell yeah." Ramel blurted. "This nigga ain't stupid by a long shot. Ya'll might be working together to get at me, who knows? If it happens, then so be it, but if you fuck up, I'll come for that ass with a vengence, Brooke."

"Boy, why you tripping? Is there anyway that I can earn your trust, while still keeping things on a professional level between us?"

HELL NO! He wanted to yell, but instead said, "Yeah, just be straight up with me. Honesty is the best policy."

"You got that, Ramel." She said. "The dude Fats is a very freaky man. Pornographic wouldn't be too much of a reach to describe him. He wants this pussy bad."

"You're a cold-blooded slut."

Brooke laughed.

"Whatchu' gathered from talking to him... I mean, what type of time is he on?"

"It's really too early to tell. He's either a fat freak or he's a natural born trickery artist."

"I betchu' a hundred bucks on the latter."

"We'll see if that's a good bet."

"With you on his ass, I know we will definitely find

out."

"If you keep pumping my head up, I'm going to float through the roof of my car and float away."

"Either that or your sexy ass is going to come through for me."

"I'm scared of you player-player."

You better be, bitch. I control if you live or die. Ramel thought then lied, "There's no need to be. We're on the same page now."

That's what I want you to think bitch. I'ma get your bitch-ass crushed in due time... In due time, she thought, listening to Ramel ask of her whereabouts.

"Cruising down Benning Road. I just left Eastgate."

"Did you already get Fats hook-up info'?"

"Yep."

"That's good. See, I knew you were the right chick for the job."

"Ouch!"

"Brooke, you a'ight? What's up?"

"That was my head hitting the ceiling," she joked.

"Stop playing all the time, girl! Lemme know what happens next."

"You got it, boss."

"Don't go there shawdy. We're a team."

No we're not! 'Cause I just switched sides. Brooke loved the game that she was playing. "You're right...it'll never happen again, boss." She giggled.

Ramel hung up on her...

Chapter 32
Hold Up Flat...Straight Up!

AROUND 3:45 p.m., Flat-Head and Ramel walked into Ben's Chili Bowl in the Uptown section of the city. It was one of the oldest and best fast food restaurants in D.C. It was a historic landmark not too far from Howard-U, where so many exotic black women attended.

Fray was waiting for them at a secluded booth in the back of the restaurant.

"Flat, Ramel. What's up, good men?" He greeted.

Flat found himself smiling. Ramel just watched their interaction. Fray always knew how to put Flat at ease. He was a beast with the flattery.

Flat-Head was mainly the reason why Ramel sicked Brooke on some guy that he himself didn't even know. A guy who could kill him if he ever found out about Ramel's plot to kill him. But Ramel would do it again at the drop of a dime to ensure the safety of his partner. Flat was his friend and he wanted him out of the line of fire.

It had been about three months since Ramel had seen Fray, due to the drama that he'd gotten into with Eastgate Fats.

"I see your waves are all the way up in there." Fray told Flat-Head.

Flat was sporting a low-cut Czar that he had started to brush in his whirlpool shaped waves. The whole look just murdered his roughneck, *go hard persona.*

"Fray, you know my shit is model material. Straight up!" Flat-Head said. "Not that I really give a fuck, but I gotta stay fly for these bitches out here, 'cause they choosing again."

Fray shrugged. "I'm just glad you're home, 'cause we got some shit to handle and some major cash to get."

"Sounds good to me. Let's talk over some grub. I'm hungry than a muthafucka."

They ordered their food, then Fray and Flat talked about the current affairs and the wicked ways of D.C. After glancing at his watch, Flat-Head cut the bullshit and got to the nitty-gritty.

"Fray, enough of the preliminary shit." Flat looked Fray in the eyes. "What's really on your mind, moe? You know I'm with you on whatever. Straight up!"

For the next few minutes, Fray told Flat and Ramel what he knew about Eastgate Fats and how their beef wouldn't end until one of them was sleeping peacefully in Harmony Cemetary.

Then Fray asked his two young soldiers to fill in as many blanks as they possibly could on a way to attack Eastgate Fats and get him out of the picture for good. Fray wanted to know what kind of niggas they were and what kind of plans they had to exterminate his beef.

As was his style, Flat-Head started rambling on about *going* up in Eastgate Projects on some Rambo killing type shit without a plan.

"I got something better in the makings." Ramel interrupted.

"What?" They asked in unison, looking at Ramel like he was crazy.

"I got somebody on Eastgate Fats as we speak."

"Who, nigga?" Flat asked.

Ramel continued pleasantly and matter-of-factly. "I probably just affirmed the belief that broads are never to be trusted. You know the broad that we snatched a while back?" Ramel looked at Fray, who nodded with a suspicious look. "I put her onto Eastgate Fats. Matter of fact, she just called me, telling me that she made contact with the nigga."

"I don't really like that kind of easy trickery myself." Flat-Head blurted. "I mean, it takes all of the fun outta going through a nigga hood and shutting shit down. Straight up!"

It was just the sort of stupid ass *go hard* shit that Ramel had expected Flat-Head to say. Flat continued to yap recklessly before looking at Ramel. "Ay, you getting soft, Ramel.

109

Using bitches to do your dirty work has never been good in my book. It's weak and it's not proper."

Fray looked up from his bowl of Chili Fries.

"Hold up, Flat. Shawdy might be on to something. That's how I hustle, anyway. Fats is so wicked on the beefin' tip, he'll never suspect a pretty chick with a big butt and a smile to be his enemy. And that, my lunchin' friend, will be his undoing."

$ $ $

The 5'8", bald headed, dark-skinned man turned his face away as Fray, Ramel and Flat-Head left the restaurant. They were so close that he could smell the strong heat of the leftover onions seeping from Flat's mouth. It was a dangerous moment and a grave mistake on their part.

The Bald Man had been following and watching Flat-Head everyday since his release from the court building. The man was sure he'd catch Flat alone and handle what he'd been paid handsomely to do.

But he could never get close to him. He was always with somebody. The Bald Man figured it would be just a matter of time before Flat-Head slipped up; and he would be right there to make sure he never got up. Flat's days of living were numbered, which was all that the Bald Man was concerned about.

Time passed. The Bald Man stabbed at the Italian Sausage with a fork. His mind allowing for the various six million ways to kill to cloud his thinking. The man looked back over his shoulder where Flat and his cronies had just left. *He's certainly a wild-one*, the Bald Man thought. *He kind of reminds me of--*.

"Excuse me," came a voice over his shoulder.

The Bald Man turned and saw a middle-aged black woman with shoulder length sandy-blond hair. She was sporting a turtleneck, tight jeans and some calf-high leather boots. Her outfit was seriously clinging to her like a second skin.

The Bald Man glanced at her, not saying anything,

110

waiting for her to speak her peace and keep it moving. She put her hand on the empty stool next to him.

So much for wishful thinking, he thought, shaking his head.

"Is this seat taken?" she questioned.

DO YOU SEE ANYBODY IN IT? He wanted to yell, but smiled and replied, "I don't think so."

She flashed a cheesy grin and sat down, invading his nose with way too much cheap perfume.

"It's hard to believe there could be a vacancy next to such a handsome man," she said while positioning her forearm on the bar. She leaned into him. "Can I buy you something else to eat, or maybe a drink?"

"I haven't finish this meal yet."

"That's okay, I'll wait." She said, nodding confidently.

You're trying too hard lady. I'm not the one. The Bald Man mused.

"I'm quite sure you'll want some desert after the meal, huh?" She smiled and rubbed his thigh.

The Bald Man threw her a flirtatious smile. She smiled back. The Bald Man then moved and knocked his plate over into her lap.

"Oops, my bad. I'm cool on the desert though," he said and quickly got up and walked away, heading for the exit.

"YOU SICK BASTARD!" The middle-aged woman shrieked in anger.

The Bald Man left the restaurant while the angry woman remained ranting and cursing him out.

$ $ $

Convinced that Flat-Head was a good distance away, the Bald Man headed for Linda Pollin Projects, where Flat's father resided. He figured it was his best chance to catch the youngster who had a $35,000 bounty on his head.

Nothing was going to deter him from getting paid for such an easy task -- not even a sexy middle-aged woman who was trying to throw her pussy on him.

111

Always business first, then pleasure, the Bald Man thought as he drove towards his destination....

Chapter 33
Pimpin' Ain't Easy

RAMEL NEEDED TO GET OUT OF D.C. FOR AT LEAST A few hours. Fortunately, he had somewhere to go.

The traffic was light heading due south on 1-95. About an hour south of D.C. all that changed. An eighteen wheeler had jackknifed and collided with a Greyhound bus and two cars, backing everything up for miles, and Ramel was reminded why he always chose to stay in the city. You could die anywhere these days. Still, he reasoned it was well worth the risk of driving to get away from the drama in the city.

After meeting with Fray and Flat and having the talk with Brooke, Ramel wanted a little sex in his life. Something to stabilize and relax him for a minute. Taking the drive down to Portsmouth, Virginia, felt good. So did spending the night with his new girlfriend, Lisa Valentine. She was a college student that he met while shopping in Georgetown with Flat several months ago.

He'd been careful in grooming her, because he saw the potential bread winner in her. Ramel gave her just enough sex, encouragement and emotional support to keep her wanting more of him. *Pimpin' wasn't at all easy, but it was necessary*, Ramel reasoned.

"Hey, baby! Boy, you don't know how much I miss you." Lisa said, greeting Ramel in the foyer of her Back Bay Brownstone. A gift from her rich parents.

She held Ramel in her arms, kissing all over his lips and face, then his cheeks, his neck. Only to do the whole routine all over again.

Yeah, she misses me, Ramel thought. "I'm almost tempted to believe you." Ramel teased, squeezing her soft behind.

Lisa stood 6'2" without her heels on. She possessed a Tyra Banks super-model frame, with a cute round face. She could pass for the R&B singer, Toni Braxton's taller twin sister. Lisa was a bonafide stallion for real. And Ramel was glad that she was all his.

"I thought you forgot all about me. You haven't called me in a week and you're down here around all these sports playing dudes. I thought they had your mind occupied," he whined, playing on her ego.

"Not in a million years, babe. Now, how could I ever forget about this?" She whispered, fondling his crotch. "And these? And this?" She asked in between showering him with kisses.

"Now I believe you," he smirked.

They continued to kiss and kid each other all the way up the stairs and into her master bedroom. Their clothes littered the floor and their bodies sweated while they made passionate love. They fulfilled each other that day and again in the early evening to the soft love ballads of Sade and Brain McKnight.

The farthest either of them strayed from the bed was when Lisa ran to meet the delivery guy with their Soul Food take-out orders.

They ate mustard greens, candy yams, fried pork chops smothered in gravy and macaroni and cheese while cuddling and watching *'How To Be A Playa'*. Ramel respected and admired Bill Bellamy's acting skills in that film. He portrayed one of the smoothest *Playas* he'd ever seen on film to date. By the time Bill Bellamy was sexing his little sister's best friend, Lisa was asleep.

Ramel waited patiently. When he finally heard that little moaning snoring sound that Lisa made, he slid out of bed and down the hallway. Once inside her office, Ramel sat at her desk and booted up her computer. She trusted him enough to give him her password. *Lucky him.*

Everything went smoothly indeed. Ramel got into her offshore bank account easily, took a tour and saw what Lisa's parents had put away for her for a rainy day. Nearly $2.5

million.

You in the door now, slim! Whatever you do, keep her on your team. She's a definite plus for your bankroll. What would Bill Bellamy do with a broad like Lisa? Ramel talked to himself. *He certainly would've milked the well until it dried up, then moved on to bigger and better chances at stacking big-faces,* Ramel thought, unable to contain the huge smile invading his face. He'd hit the jackpot with Lisa....

Chapter 34
Brooke's Love

RAMEL AND LISA WASN'T THE ONLY COUPLE THAT was getting freaky in between the sheets. In the wake of her scheming with Eastgate Fats, Brooke concentrated the rest of the day on various ways of making her mate have multiple orgasms.

From the kitchen to the bedroom, Brooke was able to accomplish a lot with her tongue over Pepa's excited body and hard nipples.

Pepa's pussy was creaming by the time they reached the bedroom. Luther Vandross' *Here and Now* crooned softly from the stereo as Brooke reached and pulled down Pepa's thongs. She slid her hand between Pepa's slick thighs and Pepa eagerly spread her legs.

"Aah... Mmmm..." Pepa moaned, biting her bottom lip as Brooke massaged her cunt with the edge of her palm.

"You like that, boo?" Brooke whispered, then started working on Pepa's slick clitoris.

"Mmmmm, yesss, baby...Yesss!" Pepa shrieked as her pussy lips became swollen and her sex-honey literally dripped out of her like a leaky faucet. "I, la-la-love you, boo." Pepa huffed as Brooke stroked her labia, then worked her fingers into her hot fuck-hole.

Pepa thrusted up at her and Brooke entered her with two, then three fingers. Pepa began taking Brooke's clothes off while Brooke masturbated her into a fourth orgasm.

Pulling off Brooke's bra, Pepa went for her yellow thongs and slid them off quickly. Brooke's beautiful dark-brown body laid before Pepa like a pleasure chest full of erotic delights. Pepa stroked Brooke's shoulders, then cupped her breasts, all the while grinding her thigh in between Brooke's legs, causing a combustible friction.

"Guuurrrl.... That's ma-my spot." Brooke moaned as Pepa pinched her nipples and slid her big toe inside her love-oven.

Pepa felt Brooke's large buds grow between her fingertips and she felt her big toe getting wet. Next Brooke began trembling with excitement while she worked her magic on her.

Brooke took Pepa's face and turned it toward her. She leaned down and kissed Pepa full on the lips. Their tongues met and the warmth flowed between them. They stood with their naked bodies pressed together.

Pepa reached down between Brooke's legs and cupped her pussy. Entering Brooke with her finger, Pepa started banging her.

"Aaah-aaah... Aaaahh... Shit gurrrll... Mmmmm...." Brooke moaned as Pepa's sensitive fingers delicatedly probed her inner most secret garden.

Brooke quivered with ultimate pleasure, time after time, while Pepa's fingers and tongue teased her unmercifully. She could feel the fourth wave of an orgasm building up deep inside, getting ready to explode.

"Right there Pep... Ra--ra--right there... It's ca-ca-ca-CUMMMINNGG!" Brooke shrieked as her love-gunk showered Pepa's penetrating fingers.

In that instant, Pepa dived between Brooke's legs and begun sucking out her love juices. Brooke started to feel like Pepa was the only one for her. And she planned to keep it just that way.

"I love you, Pepa... And I'll kill and die for you."

Pepa didn't say anything. She just continued pleasuring her lover, figuring her tongue loving was bringing out Brooke's sudden and crazy outburst, proclaiming her love.

Moments later, after they climaxed together and began cuddling, Brooke squeezed Pepa roughly and flipped her around. Stradling Pepa's thighs, Brooke leaned down and gave Pepa a soft kiss on the forehead, whispering, "If you ever cheat on me again with Ramel, I'll kill him ... then, I'ma kill you... Pepa, it's not a threat, it's a promise."

Pepa forced a smile. Those were the moments that hurt the most, when it seemed like they were actually consumating their love for each other. Pepa knew it was too good to be true, though inevitably, almost self-destructively, she knew there was never any point in arguing with her. Pepa knew instead to agree with the crazy woman who worshipped the ground she walked on, because she didn't want to hurt her or get hurt physically by her.

After all, Pepa didn't know exactly what Brooke was really capable of and she didn't want to find out....

Chapter 35
Surprise Nigga!

FLAT-HEAD ALWAYS WONDERED WHAT IT WOULD FEEL LIKE TO LOOK into the barrel of a loaded gun and now he knew. The gun was a black Glock 10mm and it was aimed at his left eye.

Flat observed the scene *out of body*, as if it were happening to a guy with a better sense of humor.

I wonder if this is one of them Eastgate niggas, or is he just out here to rob a muthafucka? Flat thought, scolding himself for getting caught slipping.

Holding him at point-blank range was a stocky pencil-brown complexioned teenager with cornrows. He looked more angry than him. He was about fourteen years old, showing just a shadow of a mustache and his brown eyes were jittery with malice. The gun aiming youth kept shifting his weight in his big black Timberland boots, standing around 5'9" in baggy jeans and a black Polo flight jacket.

Flat had froze in place when he came home and found the gun wielding youngster standing there. His angry expression suggested that he'd probably shot plenty of young African Americans in the streets.

"You don't really wanna do this moe. Straight up!" Flat-Head said with apparent calm.

The kid's long fingers trembled on the gun's cross-hatched grip, and his other hand stayed inside his jacket as if he was hiding another gun. Flat had evidently been accosted by a rookie robber. Unfortunately, the Glock was an All-Star.

"I live right here, moe. Whatchu' gonna do? Shoot me right here in front of my house?"

"What?" The teen barked, his eyes flickering with

119

madness.

"I'm broke slim. Straight up!" Flat raised his hands slowly, fighting back the instinct to run.

He'll shoot me in the back if I take off on his ass. Bitch-ass nigga, Flat thought, looking at the small walkway. He knew he'd never make it to the front door before the gun went off.

Maybe I can talk my way out of this shit. If he wanted to kill me, I'd be dead already, Flat-Head thought. He wasn't quite ready to die, so he began, "Listen moe, you don't wan—"

"SHUT THE FUCK UP!" The teen's eyes flared and he wet his lips with a large dry tongue.

Flat knew that look. It was undecisive and thoughtful at the same time. He knew the youngster was trying to decide what to do.

Flat did as he was told. Holding his hands up, his thoughts raced ahead. None of this was supposed to be happening. *Not now!* Flat had returned home that night to meet his father. The meeting was so routine and safe that Flat never thought he had to walk from his car to his house with his gun out, ready to spark a nigga.

"I GOT THE BITCH-NIGGA, FATS!" The teen yelled over his shoulder, into the dark shadows with much confidence.

Flat-Head recognized the nickname immediately and almost shitted on himself. He knew he wasn't getting out of this situation alive. He couldn't go out without a fight. He had to do something.

"EASTGATE! AY', EASTGATE! WHERE YOU AT?" The teen yelled, half turning away and Flat seized his only chance.

Flat-Head grabbed the barrel of the gun and twisted it upward. "Whose the bitch-nigga now?" Flat growled as they fight for control of the gun.

"REGGO!"

At the same time that Flat-Head's father opened the door the gun went off and his whole world exploded...

"DAD, WATCH OUT!" Flat-Head shouted as the gun erupted.

The barrel seared his palms. The shot split his eardrums.

The teen wrenched the gun back, yanking Flat off of his feet. Simultaneously, another shot rang out. Not from the Glock. Yet it was too close to be his Pop's gun. Flat's mind was working at light-speed as he looked past the teen.

Eastgate Fats, garbed in all black, was shooting at Flat's father from the walkway.

"NOOOOOOOOO!" Flat-Head screamed, grappling for the Glock. Flat glimpsed at his father as he fell backwards, grimacing with pain. Flat's arms flew open like a marionette's, throwing the gun from his hand.

"NOOOOO, POP! NOOOOOOOOO!" Flat screamed louder as Fats kept shooting from the side of the walkway. A second gunshot, then a third and a fourth burst into Mr. Belle's chest, exploding the grey colors of his sweater.

Tears fell from Flat-Head's eyes as his father's jerking body fell to the concrete and bounced on impact.

Flat-Head's heart hiccupped with fear and he yanked harder on the gun. The teen kicked him in the groin and Flat doubled over, gasping for air. He released the gun and hit back. Flat connected with the teen's jacket and held on for dear life, trying to reach his on weapon.

"Get your bitch-ass up offa me!" The teen growled, hitting Flat on the head with the gun again and again.

Flat flailed and fought until a ferocious blow from the gun crumpled him to the ground. Hitting the ground, woozy and dazed, Flat heard the faraway screams of a police siren and a voice shouting, somewhat panic stricken, "FATS, WE GOTTA GO NOW! LET'S GO MAN!"

Flat-Head laid doubled over on his side, his body was paralyzed with pain. Tears blurred his vision. He couldn't collect his thoughts. He heard footsteps and panting, then a chamber being ratcheted back.

Flat opened his wet eyes into two bottomless black wells of

a sawed-off shotgun. Hot smoke curled from the barrels, filling his nose with a burning smell. Aiming the weapon at him was Fray's foe -- Eastgate Fats.

This nigga is trying to knock my shit loose, Flat thought, rolling over in a last second effort to save himself.

"NAW SLIM!" The teen shouted. "NOT HERE. TAKE HIM WIT' US. THEM PEOPLE'S COMING!"

Suddenly Flat felt himself being lifted from the ground. As they dragged him over his father, Flat-Head saw him lying on his back with his arms still flung open wide. His eyes frozen in death and a watery red-pink bubble formed in the corner of his mouth.

NO PLEASE GOD! Flat-Head choked back tears, watching in horror as they drug him away.

If I hadn't came home, or could've got to my gun earlier, my father would still be safe and alive, he thought as the teen grabbed him by the collar and roughly shoved him inside a dark hued Ford Ecoline van.

Flat tried to escape, but was stopped by a metal linked chain being wrapped around his neck.

"You're gonna be just fine, Flat-Head. You'll see... you'll be fine. You have to be, 'cause you're the bait." Eastgate Fats whispered, then tightened the chain around Flat's neck.

Flat-Head felt his lungs screaming for air, then they gave up. As Flat-Head plunged into the abyss of darkness, he faintly heard the duo laughing about killing his father and making plans to kill Fray and everyone else who was associated with him...

Chapter 36
The Bald Man

THE BALD MAN WAS RIGHT THERE, standing outside of Flat-Head's house. He was feeling sadness and hatred. He thrived on such feelings. This was the supreme thrill for him -- letting others do his dirty work.

He felt powerful watching two unknown players beat and curse Flat; and then kill his father in cold blood. The Bald Man smelt Flat's fear. He was in a rage and shedding tears for his fallen father, yet he was powerless to do anything.

The Bald Man was counting coup. He felt in control of the situation. He even followed Eastgate Fats and the teen, who probably believed that they would rise to the top of the game one day.

What incredible hubristics on their part.

Did they truly believe they were two of the best and top criminal brains in D.C.? Of course they did. Just like so many before them thought. They all think they are so got-damn smart these days.

Well, they don't look so smart right now, committing unneccessary murder and kidnapping at the same time. They're violating every moral and code of the streets, the Bald Man thought to himself.

The Bald Man saw the van carrying his prey turn on East Capitol Street. The van cruised at a normal speed. However, Bald Man figured that the driver and his co-conspirator were angry and ready to kill his prey.

The Bald Man made certain that he had his guns out before he sped up on the van. When he eased up along side of the van he felt his adrenaline pumping at an all time high.

This was the moment.

Soon as the Bald Man lowered his window and prepared to fire his weapon, he spotted a police cruiser sitting at the intersection of Benning Road and East Capitol Street.

"You're so lucky, gentlemen. I had you with your blinders on." The bald killer-for-hire whispered, easing his gun onto his lap. "But luck only goes so far. I'll be right there smiling when it runs out." The Bald Man continued mumbling, staring at the van.

The Bald Man took a deep breath before making a left turn, following the van up Benning Road....

$$$

The bald killer watched as they got out of the van and roughly ushered Flat towards the back of an abandoned building in Eastgate Projects.

Once they entered the building's hallway, they drug Flat up a series of stairs, trying to make his ordeal as painful as possible. Flat came out of his semi-coma and again struggled for his life.

The teen, known around Eastgate Projects as Nut, tussled with Flat-Head. They then tumbled down a flight of stairs and came crashing onto the landing.

"BITCH-ASS-NIGGA! GET THE FUCK OFF MY MAN!" Fats snapped and slapped Flat hard on the back of the head with a .40 caliber handgun. Flat blacked out again.

They carried Flat up the stairs to the second landing and Nut pointed towards a door. Fats placed a key in the door and opened it. He turned back to Nut and gave him the all clear signal.

Once inside the apartment, Nut threw Flat roughly on the floor, then rushed into the kitchen to retrieve some duct tape.

When Nut returned, he saw Fats laying Flat-Head on a dirty sofa and pulling out a cellphone.

"Fuck is up, slim?" Nut probed.

"Chill out baby," Fats smirked. "I'ma see if we can

get some cash for this nigga. If Fray really fucks with shawdy we can get paid, and still crush his bitch-ass. Ain't no sense in crushing the bitch if it don't affect Fray. I want his ass."

"Shid', shawdy still gotta go, 'cause we crushed his father. He's gonna keep coming at us until he kills us or we kill him."

"Nut, lemme handle this."

"Do you, big boy... but I'm tell... A'ight." Nut sighed and walked towards Flat. "To each its own, slim. But I'ma still duct tape this nigga."

Placing the cellphone to his ear, Fats listened to the ringing sounds for several seconds. When someone answered, Fats smirked and looked at Nut.

"What's up, Fray? You thought it was over, huh? Guess what, I gotcha' man tied up in a Eastgate basement," Fats giggled. "Face it, bitch nigga. I got the upper hand now. So listen and listen good..." Fats began giving Fray instructions, causing Nut to howl with laughter while he binded Flat-Head with duct tape...

Chapter 37
Wrong Number

CHILLING IN A MARRIOT ON THE OUTSKIRTS OF THE CITY, Fray laid in bed naked, ready to get his freak on with a light-hued college beauty from Virginia Beach. When his cell phone rang he sucked his teeth irritably.

"Don't let that interrupt you, boo." Fray groaned and quickly shoved his dick inside her torrid mouth before answering the phone. He answered, "Speak on it," he said, watching her suck on his rigid member while cupping his hairy balls.

"What's up, Fray? You thought it was over, huh? Guess what, nigga? I gotcha' man tied up in a Eastgate basement. Face it, bitch-nigga. I got the upper hand now." Fray listened to Eastgate Fats' ranting and placed his hand on the woman's head, urging her on as if she was going to stop sucking.

"Listen, and listen good... If you want to see ya' man alive again, I want a million dollars dropped off in Eastgate in two days."

After hearing his foe's demands, Fray knew that he had to hurry up and hit Fats before he got to someone he really cared about.

"You hear me, bitch-nigga?" Fats growled, breaking into Fray's thoughts.

"Ay', I'm sorry bruh, but you got the wrong number.... And you definitely got the wrong nigga, with that weak-ass shit," Fray snarled, knowing it was wrong to cross Flat-Head during a crucial life and death moment. Fray closed his eyes and eliminated Flat from his thoughts as if he never existed. Then Fray started concentrating on giving his *date for the night* some thick love gunk to drink on....

126

Chapter 38
The Murder Scene

RAMEL DIDN'T SLEEP MUCH THAT NIGHT. He had some awful nightmares about Lisa leaving him before he could get his hands on her cash. He also dreamed about the beef back in D.C.

Early the next morning, he had to sneak off to the City before Lisa got up, and while the house was still dark. He didn't even get to say goodbye, and Ramel didn't like that. However, he did leave her a little love note, thanking her for the freaky love sessions.

Such a caring boyfriend, right?

Ramel drove back to the City with Scarface, 2-Pac and Biggie Smalls on the CD changer, which was some good company for the trip and whatever laid ahead.

It seemed that major threats were being thrown in his partner's direction. And since being shot, Ramel's paranoia level had shifted dramatically, and he wasn't about to sit back and let someone shoot him again... He was going after them first.

His first call was to Brooke. He asked her to come out and meet him over Flat's house. Then he sped towards D.C. HOV Lane brought him straight through.

When Ramel reached the parking lot outside of Flat-Head's house, there was bright yellow "DO NOT CROSS" crime scene tape and dry blood everywhere outside of Flat-Head's front door.

Ramel's heart sank, already figuring that something terrible had happened to Flat. Standing at the door, he could hear the burping murmurs of nosey people congregating around the crime scene.

Ramel walked around the house before sneaking inside. Suddenly he felt dizzy. A white chalk outline of a big body was on the floor. It was too big to be Flat-Head's body. Ramel shook his head. He knew then that something terrible had happened there.

Ramel began crying during the search of Flat-Head's bedroom, but was able to choke back the tears. He needed to be as clear and focused as possible when he met Brooke.

Ramel couldn't help noticing Flat-Head's things; his style, his bedroom decor. On top of his bureau was three black fleece binded notebooks. After opening them and going through them, Ramel figured that they were Flat's book of rhymes. On one of the books, the headline stated, "The Realest Shit I Ever Wrote!"

Ramel took Flat's three books of rhymes and jumped out of the window that led back to the alleyway. His car sat at the end of the alley. It was easy to tell that someone had been murdered there.

But who? Was the question.

The police crime scene tape centered around the house. The Murder Scene, it had happened right there.

When Ramel reached his car, he saw Brooke sobbing and he went to her.

"What's wrong with you?"

"I didn't wanna tell you this over the phone," she sniffled. "But something crazy happened over here last night. Pepa told me that Eastgate Fats called Fray last night and told him that they got Flat-Head, and that they want a million dollars for his safe return. Flat-Head's father, Mr. Belle, got killed last night. I guess he was trying to stop the kidnapping."

When Ramel heard that he completely lost it. His right hand flew to his face as if it had a mind and will of its own. Ramel's legs buckled badly. His entire body shook.

Brooke's voice was like an echo-chamber ringing inside his head, *they got Flat-Head and they want a million dollars for his safe return. Flat-Head's father, Mr. Belle, got killed last night.*

"Ramel, baby are you okay?" Brooke asked, choking back a smile. She wanted to laugh in Ramel's face so bad right then that it tingled her insides. It was the best revenge she ever thought of. Just watching him suffer and feel pain; she loved every minute of it.

"Yeah...yeah, I'm ca-cool." Ramel said in a low voice. "But I'll feel a whole helluva lot better soon as you gimme Fats. I want to kill him for this...and I will."

Not if I can help it, Brooke thought before walking him to his car....

Chapter 39
A Simple Pawn

IT WAS STILL A LITTLE EARLY, Eastgate Fats was tired and bored from sitting in the abandoned apartment babysitting a useless piece in his quest for revenge.

He woke Flat-Head up with the intentions of releasing him, hoping this move would lead him to Fray. Flat-Head was ugly and something in his swollen eyes said that he was sneakier than he expected, but he felt he had to take that chance. Fats often thought about Brooke, she was something to hold on to for furture set-up ventures -- guys that he wanted to kill.

"I just did this to show your young-ass that you're fucking with a snake." Fats admonished as Nut covered Flat-Head's eyes with duct tape.

And you just signed yo' death warrant, fat bitch. 'Cause if you let me go, I'm coming back harder than ever to kill your fat-ass, Flat thought.

"Ya' man, Fray hung up on me when I told him to give me a million dollars for you."

He ain't do shit wrong. I would've done the same shit, Flat thought, feeling someone pushing him foward.

"So young buck, you're not even worth my time. When you hook up witcha' man, you should kill that scared-ass-nigga for leaving you out there to die." Fats said and kicked Flat in the ass.

"AAAAARRRRRMMMMPPPPHHHH! GGGRRRRRR!" Flat-Head yelled angrily through the duct tape. He tumbled down the flight of stairs still bound by the duct tape...

Chapter 40
Need Some Help, Slim?

OUTSIDE OF THE ABANDONED BUILDING, The Bald Man spotted his prey stumbling towards a car with duct tape covering his eyes.

That's strange, the Bald Man thought, knowing things weren't supposed to turn out this way. The two unknown players were supposed to unknowingly do his dirty work and all he'd have to do was collect his $35,000.

But Flat-Head was still alive.

Now The Bald Man was flaming mad.

Easing out of his sedan, the Bald Man strolled over to Flat and stood in front of him.

"GOT-DAMN! You look like you need some help, slim?"

Flat nodded, mumbling something under the strip of duct tape that covered his mouth. He was so happy about being alive and receiving some help. All Flat could think about was revenge for his father.

Flat was semi-blinded after the strip of duct tape was ripped from his eyes. Then the strip came off of his mouth.

Without asking who his savior was, Flat-Head began thanking the stranger that stood before him.

"Don't sweat it, slim. If I can help someone, I will, which is why I'm here. I have to help Lovy get a lil' revenge. Remember you stabbed and beat his ass down Oakhill?" The bald killer asked, all the while easing out his compact semi-automatic .40 caliber.

Before Flat could react or respond, the Bald Man shot him in the face.

The impact of the Rhino-head bullet hit Flat-Head in the forehead, knocking him to the ground. The bald killer shot Flat three more times in the head just to make sure that he was dead. Pausing for a minute to see if anyone was looking, the killer backed away from Flat-Head's body. He then jogged to his car and drove off in the early morning traffic.

The only witnesses to his crime that he didn't see, were Eastgate Fats and his young partner in crime, Nut...

Chapter 41
The Drive-By

THE RIDE TO EASTGATE PROJECT WAS A TERRIFYING and angry one for Fray and Ramel. It was still hard for Ramel to swallow the fact that Flat was dead. How could they do that to him? Didn't they know that Flat-Head was locked up when their beefing began? So they had to know that he wasn't involved in any way.

Ramel felt that they had done that shit to send a spiteful message to Fray, that was a huge mistake on their part...*fatal.*

Ramel wanted to fire a thousand questions at Flat's killers, but it was impossible. Lately, he'd found himself thinking of nothings but killing the niggas who murdered his buddy.

"When we get there, we riding through and hitting anything that's moving out there." Fray said as the nose of his car turned into the boundaries of Eastgate Projects.

Ramel gave the AR-15 a quick glance over before cocking it and lowering the window.

A group of teens and men were congregated in the parking lot, having fun, unaware that death in the form of Ramel was stalking them.

Soon as they got within ten feet, one guy turned and locked eyes with Ramel just as he leaned out of the window.

"DUCK YA'LL! IT'S A DRIVEBY! IT'S A HIT!" He yelled as Ramel opened fire on the crowd.

Horrific screaming, return gunfire and screeching car tires filled Ramel's eardrums. He continued firing and watching as bodies fell. Fray sped away from the scene...

$ $ $

133

AFTER SURVIVING THE DRIVE-BY SHOOTING, Nut figured it was some of Flat-Head's homies retaliating. Nut found himself turned on, but figured it may be the adrenaline rush from merely escaping death.

Nut opened his cellphone and punched the speed dial button. When he heard the familiar voice, Nut started speaking.

"Guess what, slim?" Nut asked and didn't give Fats a chance to say *what*, before continuing. "Them bitch-ass Linda Pollin niggas just came through here shooting up shit...I'm mad as e-muthafucka'."

"WHAT!" Fats gasped. "I'll be around there in a few minutes."

"A'ight, slim. You already know what time it is too. Bring all the big shit you got with you. It's world war three." Nut said, then hung up and looked around.

The drive-by had punished several people in the crowd. There were bodies and blood everywhere that Nut looked. Nut reluctantly ran away from several of his dead friends who'd gotten caught slipping. Their glassy, red tinted eyes were staring right up at him as he ran by, but they saw nothing and never would again...

Chapter 42
What's Beef?

FLAT-HEAD'S DEATH and the murder of several men and women courtesy of Ramel's angry retaliation sparked a deadly neighborhood beef between Eastgate Projects and Linda Pollin Projects.

Innocent lives were being claimed by gun violence every night during the first month of the beef. After two eight year old kids were killed by stray bullets the Mayor put his foot down.

The Mayor, along with the Police and National Guard, began implementing a 9:00 p.m. curfew in those neighborhoods for everyone who was under eighteen years of age.

During those nights, Ramel stayed cuddled up with Lisa down in Virginia, and kept tabs on Eastgate Fats by way of Brooke. Fray went into hiding, and told Ramel to call him whenever he was ready to ride down on Eastgate Fats and end this senseless beef.

So Ramel decided to spend some quality time with Pepa; not only because she begged him to, but because of the $1,500 she paid him. They were just coming back from Mazza Gallery after doing a little shopping when Ramel ran into the same dude that he'd shot at in Eastgate over a month ago.

"Pepa, go upstairs now, and don't stop and talk to nobody. I'll be up there in a few minutes."

"Why you can't come now, Ramel? Brooke is gone for the day," she whined loudly, causing a scene. The guy that Ramel had shot at looked their way.

When they locked eyes, all Ramel saw in his was anger and death...

NUT WAS HANGING AROUND VALLEY GREEN PROJECTS waiting to purchase a few bottles of liquid P.C.P. from his buddy, Demo, who he'd been cool with since his days of incarceration at Oakhill Juvenile Detention Center.

Known for being violent in the streets, the 15 year old Nut earned his nickname by acting crazy at any given second. After beating a double homicide at trial and pleading guilty to possession of a Street Sweeper Shotgun, Nut thought he was invincible. Even the hustlers and killers housed in D.C. Jail knew about Nut. It seemed that the whole system was filled with tales of Nut's wild juvenile shootings and killing. Nut would blast anybody that rubbed him the wrong way.

While waiting for Demo, Nut pushed up on a dark-skinned beauty who resembled a darker version of the R&B singer Ashanti.

Whispering something nasty in her ear, Nut palmed her soft behind, and to his surprise, he saw the guy that shot at him and killed four of his friends during a drive-by. Nut watched as the guy talked to a female from the driver seat of a burgundy Tahoe.

Pushing the female aside that he was just hugging, Nut pulled out a big gun and aimed at the car.

It's my lucky day, Nut thought, smiling before he unleashed a volley of shots at his target.

The bullets that were destined to destroy his target quickly chined into Pepa's flesh. Ramel quickly returned fire through the passenger side window. Nut ducked and grabbed a nearby toddler for a shield. Ramel used that time to start the engine and quickly backed out of the parking lot.

"Ramel... I'm getting cold..." Pepa moaned. "Why is it so cold, Ramel? Please... Please help me."

"I got you Pepa, don't worry about a thing." Ramel said, softly. All the while keeping his eyes on Nut, who was running towards the truck still shooting like a madman.

"Bitch-ass-nigga!" Nut yelled, then dashed towards his

car in hopes of pursuing his foe. Nut knew how important it was to take out all enemies. It was a matter of life and death.

As Nut sped away, he watched cautiously for any signs of the police. While driving he pushed a few buttons on the CD player, his favorite rapper's smooth lyrics came blaring out of the speakers.

What's beef? Beef is when you need two gats to walk the streets... Beef is when you need two gats to go to sleep... Beef is when I see you--guaranteed to be in I.C.U... One moe' time, what's beef? Nut sung along with The Notorius B.I.G. while racing to catch up to the burgundy Tahoe.

For a second, Nut's mind traveled off to the woman he'd just shot and the kid he'd used for a protector shield...Then back to the music.

Since he was still alive, Nut felt that his actions were justified, and it gave him another chance to take out his enemies...

What's Beef?

Chapter 43
Fires of Revenge

SEVERAL HOURS LATER, Brooke called Ramel crying and cursing him out. She blamed Ramel for what happened to Pepa. After finally calming her down, Ramel learned that Pepa was paralyzed from the waist down. Two bullets severed her spine. That really fucked Ramel up because he somewhat felt responsible for Pepa's plight. Who would have known that the guy would just open fire like that around a bunch of innocent people?

"That's why you gotta hurry up and gimme Eastgate Fats, so I can end this beef." Ramel told her.

"I'M WORKING ON IT GOD-DAMN-IT!" She shrieked into the phone. And through all the crying and sniffles, Ramel could hear the pain in her voice.

Her lover was hurt bad, so he could imagine the pain she was enduring right then; which made Ramel excuse her disrespectful outburst.

"Brooke, I know you're going through it right now, but please, you have to work a lil' faster, boo. I want to hurt this muthafucka' like he's hurting you."

"I'll do what I can, bye." She sniffled and hung up.

Ramel called Fray and told him what happened earlier. He suggested that Ramel go into hiding, at least until Brooke carried out her part of the mission.

"That sounds proper, slim. I'ma hit you up later on, aiight." Ramel said while turning a stolen Honda Accord off of East Capitol Street and onto Benning Road. He was a short distance from the Eastgate Projects.

"Okay shawdy, I'm gone. Be safe." Fray said before hanging up.

Ramel drove at a regular speed, anticipating getting some revenge for Pepa and his fallen brethen--Flat. Ramel had to retaliate quickly before they got prepared for any unwanted drama.

It was a little after 10 p.m. and the block was packed with drug addicts, hustlers and women. The Honda Accord's windows had dark tints on them, so nobody could see him; but he saw them.

Especially the fat man sitting on some milk crates with two young men. They were sitting ducks.

Ramel parked on a quiet side street and got out. Dressed in all black army fatigues and matching Nike track shoes, Ramel was ready for war. He pulled the fitted cap low over his eyes, walking towards their hood with both hands in his pockets.

Ramel's nerves were on fire! And he was trembling like a black man at a Klu Klux Klan rally. Yet he was hellbent on making somebody pay for his pain, Pepa's pain and Flat-Head's death.

He noticed that nobody had paid much attention to him. Ramel guessed that it was due to all of the traffic coming through the area. Men were competing for drug sells and the female's attention. All oblivious to death easing up closer on them.

"Ay', ya'll know who got that crunchin' Boat?"

Before trey could direct him in the right area to buy some P.C.P., somebody called his name.

"AY' FATS! SOMEBODY WANNA SEE YOU AROUND THE CORNER!"

Without a word, Eastgate Fats stood up, then began walking away.

Fuck! Don't blow this golden opportunity! You got him! Ramel told himself as Fats turned his back and said, "Them scared-ass-niggas over Simple City got some boat sho--"

Before he could finish, Ramel whipped out two pistols. Turning, Ramel let off two shots that found their marks in the foreheads of the two dudes that were sitting with Fats. Fats

139

took off sprinting like an Olympic track star. For a big guy, the fat bastard was quick and very light on his feet.

Ramel gave chase, throwing shots at his back in the middle of Eastgate Projects. Finally, Fats fell by a car, but Ramel had ran out of bullets. Realizing the danger that he was now in, Ramel sprinted back to the car. He heard more gunshots and automatically knew that they were for him.

Pulling off the side street, several bullets penetrated the stolen Honda, shattering the windows as he sped towards the Batcave. Looking in the rearview mirrors Ramel saw a few people helping Fats to his feet. At that moment he realized that he'd missed his best chance at killing the guy that murdered his best friend...

$ $ $

TWO DAYS LATER BROOKE GENTLY PUSHED THROUGH THE DOOR OF HER LOVER'S room at D.C. General Hospital. She tried her best to smile.

But how?

She was mad and in bad shape, and she knew it. So did anyone else who came into contact with her--the doctors, nurses and her lover's new physical therapist.

For a little while, Brooke pretended as if she had never met, nor tried to kill Ramel several weeks before. Brooke acted as if she never knew her lover was with Ramel when she got shot.

But she knew. She knew everything.

"Hey, baby. How do you feel?" Brooke asked, stroking Pepa's hair, lovingly. It knotted her stomach to see Pepa this way.

Pepa was laying on top of her green covers in a teal colored DC General Hospital nightgown. She glanced at Brooke with a blank smile and a fugitive tear slid down her cheek.

"Brooke, the doctors told me that I'll never walk again." Pepa sniffled. "I know I haven't been the best to you, but please don't leave me. Not like this."

"We're married for life Pepa. Nothing or no one will ever

140

separate us." Brooke said soothingly before hugging Pepa. She allowed Pepa to cry like a baby in her arms.

$$\$\,\$\,\$$$

The clouds hung low for most of the day, but were now beginning to clear up. However, the swirl of emotions that surged through Pepa and her lover was like sitting in the middle of a hurricane. Brooke comforted her lover as best she could.

"Pepa, don't worry baby, we'll get through this together."

Any lover would've said that at that moment. The difference with Brooke was that she actually believed it. She didn't use her eyes to see the reality of Pepa's plight. She only used her prayers and hopes. It was a force of habit. After Pepa cheated on her Brooke prayed and hoped one day that Pepa would solely depend on her, then she would have the power.

Now that she had the power, Brooke hated it and really wanted to make Ramel suffer for hurting her lover. Not to mention getting revenge for getting raped by him. She was scorned and she was determined to make Ramel feel her wrath.

"I can't live without feeling my legs. I need to walk, Brooke." Pepa cried, invading her thoughts.

Muthafucka! I'ma kill you Ramel! Brooke thought, but spoke softly to Pepa. "I know you can, baby. You can't give up that easy. I'm afraid it's gonna take a minute before you can walk again. You know... Well, you've been--"

A loud ear shattering scream started up on the floor outside of Pepa's room. The horrific cries of "NOOOOO! MY BABY'S NOT DEAD! HELP HIM PUHLEEASSE!" Penetrated the room and gave Brooke a jolt.

Brooke suddenly felt paralyzed and out of breath. The only thing working was her tears. Her facade collasped and all of the hurt and pain she held in for so long came pouring out. She didn't even care to wipe her eyes.

"I'm sorry, Pepa, but you deserved everything you got for cheating on me for the umptenth' time. You promised

141

me that you wouldn't do it no more."

For the first time, Brooke told her lover how she really felt, and revealed the news of her attempt to kill Ramel and how he had raped her. How vivid in her mind those days remained. Brooke recalled exactly what was said, everything she wore, even the smell of stale urine and liquor in the abandoned house.

"Baby, I'm sorry. I swear to God I didn't know that." Pepa gasped, feeling guilty behind Brooke's pain.

Brooke took a tissue from the bedside table. It was as if a dam had burst. Her tears, her emotions, everything came pouring out. Brooke lost control. She felt the overwhelming compulsion to talk to someone.

Brooke drew the deepest breath, coaxing her lungs to expand. Finally exhaling, she closed her eyes and spoke.

"Pepa, I'm sorry about what happened to you. I really am. I didn't mean what I just said. It was the heat of the moment, and I was mad at you for betraying me after you said that you wouldn't. And I told you to stay away from that nigga. Don't worry though, because after tonight, he'll never be able to come between us and our love again."

Brooke sprung up from Pepa's bed and ran out of the room. She burst out into the hallway, then pulled out her cellphone from her purse. Brooke dialed several digits in hopes of erasing her problems for good.

On the third ring she got the connection she wanted.

"Hello?"

"Hey Fats. I need to see you tonight. Ramel is really pressing me to set you up, so let's grant his wish."

"Whatchu' got in mind?"

"Revenge... Meet me in thirty minutes over 8th and H Street, by the lil' strip mall where the Muslims sell all the oils at. I'ma give you all the details then, okay."

"I'm already en route shawdy. But remember what I told you." He reminded her of the warning he had given her when they first met, then hung up.

"I'll never cross you, big boy. You're my only ticket to

142

getting what I want," Brooke mumbled as she closed her cellphone.

Looking back at Pepa's hospital room, Brooke wiped away the last of her tears. She then sauntered down the hallway nodding her head. Brooke's heart grew colder by the second and her blood got hotter from the consuming fires of revenge...

Chapter 44
Pussy Persuasion

THEY KISSED AND EMBRACED LIKE A COUPLE OF OVERHEATED TEENS IN THE HONEY MOON SUITE at the Marriot Courtyard Hotel in Greenbelt, Maryland. Brooke had just arrived ten minutes after Eastgate Fats.

"You're my bitch, now. Ride or die 'til the end." Fats said, holding her tight in his short arms, stroking her hair. "Once we crush these niggas, I want you to do something big for me."

Imagine that! Brooke thought, then asked, "And what's that, boo?"

"Always keep it clean and real with me, because I would hate to have to dust yo' sexy ass off." Fats spoke with a sinister leer. Brooke looked at him, confused, and broke into a grin.

"I'll be the only one you'll ever be able to count on through thick and thicker, Fats. I'm down for whatever," she replied, playfully poking him in the chest.

"Action always speaks louder than words...Always."

"Then say no more. You'll see, just watch."

"Show me something now," he said, palming her soft behind.

"Yes master," she gulped before taking his hand and leading him to the huge bed.

Pushing him back onto the bed, Brooke pulled off her blouse and turned her back to him.

"Now close your eyes," she cooed.

Fats obeyed her request. Brooke then expertly eased his jeans and underwear off. His reaction was immediate. Brooke massaged his rigid love-pole, giggling seductively.

"Okay, you can open your eyes now," she whispered.

When Fats opened his eyes Brooke was butt-naked, holding his stiff throbbing cock in her delicate hand. She licked it slowly, making sure that the head of his cock touched every inch of her gums. Then she took him whole, deep into her hot mouth.

"Damn, guurrrll!" Fats groaned, wrapping his hands around her bobbing head. His eyes were now closed again.

Brooke continued pleasuring his beefy jack-hammer. And out of nowhere, emotions hit her and tears began to well up in her eyes. Revenge was the motivating factor. The act that she was performing right then represented how she felt. It showed just how bad she wanted to see Ramel die.

Fats gave her head another squeeze.

"I see you really know how to get a nigga hooked, don't you?"

"MMMMmmmmmmmm.....," she slurped loudly, consuming his jabbing prick. Brooke then flashed a grin. "Whatever it takes, Daddy... Whatever it takes."

"I hear you. Witcho' slick ass."

"I'll never cross you, boo." She moaned, licking around his hairy balls. All the while her soft hands were busy jerking him off.

"You bet' not. Now get up here and lemme tap that ass."

They kissed. Fats lifted her gently. She felt like a feather in his strong arms. He laid her down on top of the bed and paused, watching her get up on her hands and knees.

Fats stared unblinkingly! He simply wanted to enjoy the view--her naked fanny wiggling at him. Her chunky pussy seemed to wink at him as he penetrated her slowly. Fats was in heaven, feeling her oozing slit part wide for his diving jizz-rod. Her tightening muscles tugged at his impaling love-stick, sending chills of ecstasy sweeping through his body. Fats fucked her, enjoying what he was feeling.

"Faster, boy... Faster!" Brooke demanded. They fucked feverishly, holding nothing back. Their slapping flesh and love organs interwined like a fuse.

Until finally they exploded. At least Fats did. The sexual

145

act left Brooke unsatified. Yet her acting had been played to perfection. She had justly stroked her pawn's ego.

A minute passed as they embraced. Neither one saying a word. With a deep exhale, Fats finally rolled to one side and grabbed his cellphone.

"I'm ready to smash them niggas tonight," he said while Brooke played with his limpness. "How about you?"

Brooke propped up her head with the pillow. Still massaging his dick, all the while envisioning Pepa laying helpless in a hospital bed, paralyzed and of no use to her. That really infuriated Brooke.

She clambered on top of Fats and stared into his eyes.

She easily impaled herself on his evergrowing stiffness. Brooke wondered if there was any man in the world quite like him--ready to kill for her, due to the persuasion of her P-U-S-S-Y?

"Yes, boo." Brooke finally answered softly, gyrating her pulsating cunt on his stabbing cock. "MMMmmmm... I think... I think the time has finally come... Fa... For you to ma-make that call," she moaned, speeding up her pace. Brooke was fucking her way to an orgasm and her ultimate revenge...

Chapter 45
A True Player

RAMEL LAID IN BED STARING UP AT THE CEILING, holding the thought as it were. This was probably his ticket out of the streets and it was still there for him to take. But Ramel felt like he owed it to Flat-Head to avenge his death. Yeah, he had killed a few guys, but he had not gotten the one solely responsible for his friend's death. Once Ramel got him, only then could he move on with life.

With that settled in his mind, Ramel finally began plotting his escape from the streets. Figuring what he might do and where Lisa and himself might go to live. More importantly, how he would navigate their budding relationship and control most of that money she had tucked away.

Ramel certainly knew how to get what he wanted. The question was, *was it Lisa that he wanted? And what did he want out of their relationship besides her money? Was it to prove that he could trick a rich female out of her wealth? Or to show that he could do it ten times better than the B&B singer Bobby Brown had done when he married Whitney Houston?*

Ramel told himself to snap the hell out of it. The only question that really mattered was whether Lisa could finance his dreams of putting Flat-Head's lyrics onto a CD and starting his own record label. That was his job, getting that answer.

He closed his eyes. Seconds later, they popped open. Ramel jumped out of bed and ran to his Armani Jeans hanging over the chair. He grabbed the ringing telephone out of his pocket and checked the number, hoping to see a certain string of digits.

It was Brooke!

Ramel couldn't ignore her call. She could have been calling to give him Eastgate Fats.

Be yourself Ramel, he thought before answering.

"What's up?"

"Why are you whispering?" Brooke asked as Lisa's eyes opened and looked directly into Ramel's.

Shit! He cursed under his breath.

"Because I'm in church."

"Stop playing, boy! Where you at?"

"I'm with my wife, why?"

"Because you're bullshittin'. I got the nigga for you now. He's in the shower as we speak."

"That's a good move. You sure know how to work your shit."

"Yeah, so you needs to come handle your part."

"Do you think he suspects anything?"

"No, he's thinking about fucking me."

Ramel swallowed hard on that one. Lisa sucked her teeth loudly, then rolled over in bed, turning her back to him. She was mad at him.

"You mean like, right now?" Ramel questioned.

"How else was I going to get him for you?"

Ramel laughed. "I underestimate you sometimes."

"You should. I'm harmless remember, choke-choke." She giggled, reminding him of her attempt on his life.

This bitch has a sick sense of humor, Ramel thought to himself before speaking his mind. "You still got jokes, huh? I told you off top, leave that shit alone."

"Trust me, I did," she said. "I just couldn't resist that one. You left yourself wide open for the sucker punch."

"Listen, I'ma call Fray, then we're going to come handle that B.I. It's probably our best shot to get his fat ass. What's the address?"

"Damn."

"What's up?" Ramel asked.

"I gotta go," she gasped. Ramel could hear the panic in her tone. "The big man is coming out of the bathroom."

148

"Aiight, get going. But listen. Be careful and call me back as soon as possible with that info."

"I will. Bye."

Ramel hung up, got back into bed and tried cuddling with Lisa, but she elbowed him off of her.

"Don't be that way, boo," he whispered, guiding his semi-erect penis inside her damp center. "You know I have to take care of my business right?" Ramel said, kissing the back of her neck, slow dicking her until she began backing her ass up, meeting his hard slow thrust.

"I know ... I'm sorry, boo," she moaned, tightening her pussy muscles around his jabbing shaft.

"I ja-just get sooo... MMmmmm....Ja-ja-ealous sometimes .... You don't know how much I really love you, Ramel...Oooohhh, Ramel." She huffed as he started to swell inside of her warm torrid tunnel, fucking her like it was their last day together.

He hated having to play on Lisa's emotions, but he hardly had a choice. She wanted a man to give her the things that she needed and wanted. Now Ramel was wondering if he was Mr. Right for her or simply *Mr. Right Now?* He hadn't chosen this path in life, it chose him.

Lisa was one of the most naive, gullible and sex-starved females he'd ever known. Ramel guessed that was why she was in love with him; because he could give her the dick at anytime without disappointing her. *That's what true players and dick layers do...*

Chapter 46
Having Devilish Thoughts

LISA AND RAMEL showered and made love again under the warm jets, showered again, got dressed and ate a small feast. French toast, cheese grits, bacon, eggs and various fruits.

He left Lisa all bright and full of pep. *That's what good dick does for a woman,* Ramel thought as he stared at her.

Lisa rolled her eyes and made a funny face that won his heart under the circumstances.

"I'ma see you in a few days," Ramel slid his shades on before opening the front door.

"I'll be waiting," she kissed him. "Love you."

"I love you too," he mumbled, letting her wipe her smeared lip gloss from his lips.

Soon as he pulled off, he called Fray and told him to meet up at the Verizon Center in two hours. They had to finish off Eastgate Fats, and fast!

Ramel drove into The City with Lisa heavy on his mind and Flat-Head's death burning in his heart. *Damn, I miss him. But am I throwing away something special trying to avenge my partner's death? Would I be compromising my morals, principles and the love I have for Flat-Head if I overlook the killers and let them live, so I can spend more time with Lisa and her millions?* All of this ran through Ramel's young confused mind.

The next stop was the weed-spot in Southwest on Delaware Street. Ramel bought a quarter pound of skunk from his man, Chin. Chin was an ultra-good dude that he'd met through Flat-Head. The streetvine had it that he was not going for nothing and had several murders under his belt. The two shared a few memories of Flat-Head over a few blunts of herb, which solidified his decision to avenge his man's death. Ramel knew that Flat-Head would've wanted him to. Plus Flat would've done the same thing for him.

As Ramel drove towards The Verizon Center to meet Fray, he felt the effect of the weed. He started wondering what it would feel like to finally get revenge and put this chapter of life behind him.

As he got closer to The Verizon Center, his cellphone chirped a few times. Ramel already knew who it was.

"Spit it out, Brooke."

"We right off the B/W Parkway, near Capitol Plaza Mall. The hotel sits right next to the highway. It's the only Best Western in sight. We in room 211."

"I'm on my way. Whatever you do, hold his fat ass in that room for me." Ramel hung up and sped toward his destination like an unemployed joe trying to be prompt for his first day at work....

$ $ $

RAMEL WASN'T THE ONLY ONE HAVING DEVILISH THOUGHTS OF seeking out some help to do away with his troubles. Fats was on the telephone giving Nut directions to the hotel where he'd just got Brooke to set the trap for the two snakes that wanted to bite him.

What nobody knew, but Brooke, Fats and Nut, was that the hotel's directions that they'd gave Ramel was a hotel at least several miles away from the hotel they were staying in.

After another quick sexcapade, Brooke and Fats headed out of their room to meet up with Nut at the other hotel.

While Fats drove, he kept looking at Brooke. Returning his stare with a comforting smile, Brooke noticed there was a slight squint in his eyes.

Hesitation, bordering on suspicion. Enough to make her back off with trusting him. So for the rest of the ride, Brooke played it cool... Like a girl enjoying an unexpected day of quality time with the boyfriend she just couldn't get enough of. Yet inside Brooke preceded with the caution of a wild impala watching a stalking lion from her peripheral vision, preparing to run away, so she could live to see another day...

Chapter 47
The Set Up

AFTER MEETING WITH FRAY, the two drove out Maryland to the hotel in separate cars. This was Fray's idea. He wanted to bring the element of surprise, just in case of a double-cross. After explaining how they had raped and dissed her several months ago, the possibility of a double-cross became highlighted in Ramel's thinking.

"Slim, that bitch know I'll punish her ass," he declared, not revealing what he was really thinking, which was that Fray had a good point.

"Ramel, a woman is the most vindictive and unpredictable creature on the face of this earth. You show me one man who has figured them out and I'll show you a virgin nun that's fucked more niggas than Wilt Chamberlain fucked bitches."

"There's no such thing as a virgin nun fuckin' —"

"It's impossible foolio'," he cut Ramel off. "That's what I'm trying to hip you to. We can't figure them bitches out. And we definitely don't know how this bitch is going to carry it after we dogged her out in that abandoned joint."

Fray's words danced around Ramel's head during the drive to Maryland. By the time they made it to the hotel, Ramel was telling himself to turn around and go back home to Lisa. *Leave now Ramel. Drive away, you stupid muthafucka!*

But he didn't leave. Ramel had to see this thing through.

After parking, he leaned down to retrieve his guns out of the stash spot. When he looked up he saw Fray jogging towards the hotel room.

The hotel was set up like a duplex motel, and the front desk for checking in and out rested sixty yards away from the room that Brooke had given him. The set up seemed perfect. *But who was really being set up?*

Fray what the fuck is you doing? Wait for me, you crazy son of a bitch, Ramel thought, jumping out of his truck with two pistols drawn.

Jogging towards the metal steps, Ramel glanced around at the dark and quiet surroundings before creeping up the stairs.

Soon as his foot touched the third step from the first landing, rapid gunfire invaded the quiet night. Ramel stumbled backwards a little, trying to get ready for war.

Yet nothing could prepare him for what was happening.

When he heard gunshots erupting simultaneously from two different guns, Ramel knew that the set-up was for them. Brooke had put them in a double-cross, just as Fray had predicted.

How could I be so damn stupid?

Sprinting back to his car, Ramel turned just in time to see Eastgate Fats and the guy that shot at him and paralyzed Pepa. They were running into the parking lot with their guns drawn, confirming his suspicions.

THAT BITCH SET ME UP! His mind screamed.

Easing into the truck, Ramel started the engine quickly and they began shooting in his direction.

FUCK!

Ramel ducked low and threw the truck in gear, speeding towards Eastgate Fats, who was standing in the center of his escape route, still throwing shots at the front windshield.

"Stay right there you fat bastard... Stay right there... Please, please don't move." Ramel growled, stepping on the gas pedal. The truck beared down on him like a locomotive.

Fats unleashed several more shots before diving out of the way. Ramel continued speeding out of the death trap that Brooke had set up for him.

Damn, she's wicked with it! But I got something for her ass, Ramel thought while looking in the rearview mirror. Fats and his henchmen were running towards their cars. Knowing Fray was dead, Ramel told himself that things had to come to a halt today.

He was already jumping on the highway, heading into a full circle. Ramel was actually planning to turn Fray's demise into an advantage for him. And he figured that he knew right where to start....

Chapter 48
Hazelnut Vanilla

FUELED BY RAGE, BETRAYAL, AND MAYBE EVEN A LITTLE HEARTBREAK, Ramel drove like a hungry Nascar Driver back to the hotel. He was out of his mind and seething with vengeance.

Driving along Ramel was besieged by unanswered questions. Dangerous questions! *Why did Brooke set me up? Was there really a truce between us? What was her hidden motives? And what about the sex we'd had. How did it all factor in?* The only thing that Ramel truly knew for sure was that he'd been tricked, lied to and set up by an expert.

How about that? The manipulator had just gotten manipulated.

Ramel arrived back at the hotel and went on a rampage! Stepping over Fray's corpse he snapped and started breaking expensive things all over the room.

"I'MA KILL THAT BITCH!" he yelled, hurling a chair against the wall mirror, shattering it.

Shards of glass flew everywhere.

Ramel heard the sounds of police sirens approaching the scene. Then Brooke crept out of the bathroom.

"Ra-Ramel," she gasped, apparently surprised by his presence.

"In the flesh and still alive, bitch." Ramel snarled, pulling his gun out on her. "Let's go, bitch." Ramel dragged her out of the room and beat her ass all the way to the truck.

She tried to run, but Ramel pushed her as she took off and she fell on her face.

"I'M SORRRY! PUHLEEEASSE STOOOP!" she howled as he whipped her ass. She fainted from the excitement.

As soon as Ramel got Brooke into the truck, a thousand Prince George's County Police cars converged on the scene, crowding the parking lot and his escape route.

FUCK!

Ramel vowed revenge, but the planning and plotting would have to wait. Right then he had to get out of the road block. By the time he made it to the edge of the parking lot a couple of cops were standing their with their guns out--an apparent road block. Ramel pulled Brooke close to him to make it look like she was sleeping. The move also hid the gash on the side of her temple.

The adrenaline and fear of getting caught was almost a blessing--wicked as it was. It immediately took his mind off of what made him come out there in the first place.

"Is there a problem, officers?" Ramel asked cordially.

"Yes sir, we received a call from the desk clerk stating that gunshots were going off around here. Would you know anything about that?" he asked, holding his flashlight up to Ramel's face, damn near blinding him.

"I heard them too. That's why I'm checking out so early with my wife. I didn't feel safe. But now that you're here, maybe I can go back to my room and get some shut eye before driving back home to Florida." Ramel lied quickly.

"I suggest you find another hotel, sir." He smiled. "Have a safe trip," he tilted his hat and Ramel drove away, exhaling his nervousness.

After getting away from the scene, his anger returned. It was the smell of Brooke's Hazelnut-Vanilla scent--the same scent that he smelt on her when they'd first made their pact.

Only it wasn't a pact. It was never honesty on her part. Only trickery! Ramel really thought while glancing at her unconcious frame.

He'd taken her deadly craftiness for granted. Now all bets were off. She would never cross another nigga again,

157

Ramel told himself as he sped past the Welcome to Washington, D.C. road sign. He was now heading towards the dark train tracks near Barry Farms Projects....

Chapter 49
Not Even For Fats

NUT KEPT JABBING A FINGER AT the selection button on the CD changer, jumping from one CD to another. He was riding shotgun, en route to Eastgate Projects while Fats drove. There wasn't a single song that he wanted to hear. Most of the slow FAB joints that Fats had on display made Nut want to scream.

Finally that's what he did!

"AAAAAAHHHH!"

"Nigga, what the fuck is wrong with you? You better pipe all that bamma' shit down in here." Fats raised his voice. Nut knew he was dead serious.

Nut was anxious, paranoid and fidgety, which only intensified all the P.C.P. he'd just smoked. Thinking about the guy who'd gotten away from them had left him wired and hot with anger.

When Fats' cellphone rang, Nut nearly shot his partner in crime.

"You need to leave that shit alone, Nut. For real." Fats admonished while glancing at his caller ID.

"Ay Nut, this the bitch from the hotel. She's probably mad at me 'cause we left her and a body on her doorstep." Fats snorted with laughter. "Hello?"

"Ay', you got me big boy. I admit, I never seen that one coming."

"Look, you scared-coward-ass nigga," Fats barked, almost swerving into the wrong lane. "Take it like a man. You jumped out there and came at me, you die. It's as simple as that."

Ramel instantly warmed. "My bad, gangsta. You right.

159

I just called to letchu' know, it's over. I don't want no more beef."

An outburst was needed, a good one, Fats thought.

"Well, you got it, scared-ass-nigga. What? You thought I forgot how your sucka-ass came at me in my hood? I won't stop until you laying beside you man Fray and Flat-Head up in Harmony, bitch nigga!"

With that said, Fats hung up the phone, then rolled down the window and tossed the cellphone into the street.

"What's up, slim?" Nut asked as Fats navigated his car through the back streets of Southeast.

"Ain't shit. Just that scared-nigga that got away calling. He trying to take a cop."

Nut remained silent, as if he'd somehow missed something the first time.

"What did you tell him?"

"What did I tell him?" Fats looked at Nut like he was crazy. "You must really be twisted off that shit, talking to me like that?" Fats howled with laughter.

He's mad. He only laughs at me when he's pissed, Nut thought, filing this episode into his mental bank.

It was getting harder to keep track of the things that didn't upset Fats, which meant risk. Nevertheless, Nut felt he wasn't about to change his ways to please anybody. Not even Fats. And not even if life depended on it...

Chapter 50
The Moment Of Truth

RAMEL WAS FEELING SO GODDAMNED CONFIDENT AND EXCITED that he couldn't stand it. He'd made it to the dark train tracks without being stopped. There was no fear anymore. No one scared him. Not even Eastgate Fats. Not anyone involved with this beef shit.

Ramel had a vicious plan for Brooke's double-crossing ass. A different kind of plan. The maneuver was so clever that he'd never heard anything like it.

The most commonplace part was waking her trifling ass up. He smacked her a few times and pinched her nipples roughly. Then v o i l a, s h e was woke.

Ramel listened to the bitch breathe for a delicate moment. The only other sounds that could be heard was the blaring radio. It whistled the Go-Go beats of Rare Essence Band. The truck was parked in the middle of the train tracks.

Ramel was somewhat afraid to be on these tracks where dead bodies were discovered on a daily basis. But the fear was natural and intoxicating. The fear made the moment good for him.

Ramel slipped on a pair of latex surgical gloves--the same kind of gloves that he'd used in the first murder that he'd ever committed.

He quietly wiggled Brooke's fingers, which were duct taped to the steering wheel. This was getting good to him. Ramel almost felt that it was destined for him to be there at that time.

The moment of truth!

Ramel moved very fast. Snatching the wad of duct tape from across her mouth, he then pulled out a pair of bolt cutters that he'd brought along.

Brooke's eyes widened. She tried to twist, turn and break free. Ramel loved the fact that she was scared.

"Shhhhh...." he whispered, caressing her wet cheeks before running his fingers over her face, then back and forth through her hair. She turned away from him. "It's not going to happen. Your cruddy-ass can't get away. So you can stop trying, it's becoming annoying."

Brooke said nothing. "You know why you're here, right? I'm going to explain what I plan to do to you. I'ma be straight up and precise. I'm going to torture you for betraying me tonight. I trust that you won't tell a soul about this, because you was the cause of somebody dying tonight. But if you ever do tell I'll come for your ass again and it'll be worse than tonight. I'll find you anywhere, and I will kill you and Pepa, but first I'll do much worse than that."

She nodded. At last, understanding. Threats of death was the magic needed to tame her. Perhaps it should've been used more in relationships, Ramel thought.

"Why did you set me up? Now, before you speak, pay close attention to your pretty little fingers and these wire cutters." Ramel said, rubbing the instrument across her lips. "Everytime you lie to me, one of your fingers will die. Now start talking."

He could see the fear in her eyes, which he loved.

"Ra-Ramel...I swear to God I didn't set-- AAAAAHHH! AAAAAAHHHHH!" she cried as he began cutting off her pinky finger. "STOOOOOP! I'M SORRY! PUHLEEEEEEEAAASSSEEE!" she shrieked as he hit the bone and broke off her finger. "*AAAAAAAHHHHHH! OH MY GAWD! YOU CUT MY—*" she screamed, then dropped her head to the steering wheel. Brooke was now wailing like a dying inmate in the center of a deadly prison riot.

"I've been watching and studying you bitches for a minute now. I know when ya'll are lying, and when ya'll are telling the truth. Help yo'self to live, Brooke." Ramel said soothingly, then opened a few iodize salt packets from Mc'Donalds. He sprinkled them over her fresh wound.

"AAAAAAAAHHHHH!" she yelped, slamming her

head backwards into the headrest like she'd just been shot in the head.

"I mean, we can go through this shit all night or until all your pretty lil' fingers are gone... but you will give me the answers that I want, because there's always your toes to work on."

"Okay...Okay... Please don't da-do me like that again," she huffed between sniffles, trying to get her breathing together.

"Bitch, start talking. Why did you set me up?"

"BECAUSE I HATE YOU!" she yelled, staring at him. "You stole my love away from me. Then you forced me to suck your dick. And you raped me with your buddy! What would you have done?" she cried, then looked away from him.

Before Ramel could say anything she looked back at him, directly into his eyes with a look that pleaded for sympathy. But Ramel wasn't taking her for granted anymore. *Not her!* Any other female, maybe. *But not her.*

"I would've gave you a one-way train ticket out of the city." Ramel said, then kissed her hard on the lips and exited the truck.

Then it happened!

The freight train's headlights appeared just like clockwork.

"NOOO! RAMEL, PLEASE! RAAMMEEEEEL! I'M SORRY... PUHLEEASSE HELLPPPP MEEE! I'LL DO WHATEVER YOU WANT!" Brooke yelled, still trying to break free. The industrial steel locomotive was bearing down on her.

"You told me that before. I can't fall for your lies twice." Ramel smirked while backing away. The fear was ripe in her eyes.

The train's lights were larger now and Brooke stared at her approaching death like a shocked deer caught out there on an open country road.

"Don't worry though. I'll look after Pepa for you." Ramel called, then backed away a little more. The train's warning horns blared repeatedly.

163

"HEEEELLLLLPPP MEEEEE! RAAMMMEEEEELLL! HEEELLLLLPP!" Brooke yelled repeatedly. Then microseconds later Brooke received Ramel's warning message about betraying him.

As the train made contact with the precious SUV, a massive explosion ripped through the truck and through Brooke's cruddy-ass. The fiber glass and metal structures of the SUV snapped like a piece of peanut brittle. Huge sparks and chunks of metal popped out and plummeted towards the patches of bushes and trees that surrounded the train tracks.

When the train slowed down, Ramel lit up a victory blunt, took a couple of satisfied puffs and walked away knowing that his pursuit of Flat-Head's revenge died along with Brooke in the train crash.

He had other plans for his life. Like locking down Lisa, making her fall in love with him and putting out Flat's music. Ramel planned on becoming a millionaire. So he knew that he had to just walk away from the unfinished beef he had with Eastgate Fats.

With that in mind, Ramel continued walking towards Suitland Parkway, knowing from that point on in life that there was *No Turning Back...*

Chapter 51
RAMEL TALKING

19 MONTHS LATER

I found myself strolling out to my private terrace in the afternoon sun, wearing nothing but a sly smile. I sipped from a bottle of Dom Perignon then pressed it against my cheek. I'd yet to tire of the view from my new found success. I loved the white sands of the beautiful St. Tropez Beach. The way it seemed to melt into the turquoise waters was a sight to behold and I enjoyed every minute of it. I couldn't have designed this destiny any better myself.

St. Tropez had a well deserved reputation as an exclusive vacation and hideaway spot for the Rich & Famous. I was employing the vacation part. During the day, behind Dior Homme Shades, I was a rich independent record label C.E.O. lounging by the pool. And at night, well, the way Lisa and I had been steaming up the bedroom, we never ate out at night. Room service always fed us. In fact, on some days, like honeymooners, we never left our villa. Thankfully, the spot that we stayed in also had a great room service menu for breakfast and lunch.

After the night I killed Brooke, I made it to Lisa's home early the following morning and explained my dreams of becoming a C.E.O. and putting out Flat-Head's music.

By the Grace of God, Lisa eagerly wanted to support and finance my dreams every step of the way. I stumbled at first, trying to do everything by myself. Then I turned the marketing and promotional aspects of the business over to Lisa. She was a born decision maker. The one move that made us the most money was recognizing that all small colleges in

Virginia, North Carolina and South Carolina needed new Urban *Music* for their radio stations, before any major radio stations broke the songs first. That edge helped me to get Flat-Head's songs out there into the public, thus creating No Turning Back Entertainment.

We currently have three R&B acts and superstar Hip-Hop artists on the label; which grossed my label a little over $34.8 million in record sales in the first year. That's enough money to get the president assassinated and have the Major Record Labels blowing up my cellphone daily, trying to be apart of the successful empire that Lisa and I built from ground zero.

So I was definitely where I always wanted to--RICH BITCH!

"Daddy, do you want to wear the white Versace or the white Hugo Boss linen stuff today?" Lisa called from the bedroom, bringing me back to reality.

Decisions, decisions...

"Go ahead and pick it out for me, boo." I said, looking at P. Diddy play on the jet skis with his son, Justin.

And to think, he and I both owed our success to the demise of our best-friends and the fact that we left the beef alone when we did. I would've never gained everything I have today if I would've stayed hellbent on revenge.

Lisa called me again from inside of the bedroom after placing the lunch order.

"Baby, do you realize that you're naked out there?"

"I can do that, 'cause I got money!" I said, causing her to laugh.

"Boy, bring your ass in here. I need my wake up dick."

I went back inside the villa and climbed into bed with Lisa, my fiancee, and she snuggled up against my chest.

"I love you sooo much, Ramel," she whispered, inserting my semi-erectness into her warm slit.

There was just one problem.

I couldn't get Eastgate Fats out of my head. His slick words, his ruthlessness; the way he seemed to get inside of my head after I left the street life alone. It was like he was taunting me way over in St. Tropez, all the way from D.C.

166

It made me angry. I didn't want these thoughts to affect my life. I didn't want to be sexing my fiancee, or any other woman, and be thinking about Eastgate Fats.

What the fuck is wrong with me? I don't dwell on nothing! Why start now?

"Baby, what's wrong..." Lisa asked as my dick softened inside her fuck-hole.

I snapped out of my faraway gaze. "My bad, baby-girl. I was just thinking about some unfinished business that I have back at home."

"Well, you need to stop thinking," she smiled. "I'm the only business that should be on your mind. That's what this vacation is for, relaxation. Now lay back and concentrate on another day in paradise," she said, then ducked under the sheets and took my limpness into her warm mouth.

Soon as I got into her oral pleasure, a knock at the door interrupted us.

"ROOM SERVICE!"

"COME BACK IN A FEW MINUTES!" I yelled. Lisa giggled under the sheets, trying her best to suck her way to my heart. She was trying to make me forget about my past and the dude that killed my best friend.

I can forgive... but I can never-ever forget.

EPILOGUE

EASTGATE FATS DROVE HIS MERCEDES BENZ
AROUND D.C., flying, until he was sure that no one was
following him and Nut. Not the police or the dude who'd tried
to squash the beef with him over a year and a half ago. On a
suggestion from Nut, Fats gunned the Benz up onto the
straight speedway known as the B/W Parkway, and headed north
to Atlantic City. He wanted some time away from the city.

Fats was breezing along in the luxury automobile at
a speed of 91 m.p.h. This was the life. He was totally free.
He'd gotten away with numerous murders and still remained
on top of his game. It felt good. Selling drugs was the best
thing that had ever happened to him. Fats figured he would
hang out in Atlantic City for a few days, finally meet his
connect for the latest shipment, then plan his next move on how
to monopolize the rest of Southeast.

Funny, he was thinking, *maybe it's even time for me to
quit this shit and let Nut take over things. Get me a bad
bitch, for real, and put a few babies up in her.*

The idea made Fats laugh, but he didn't dismiss it. Stranger
things had happened; like him escaping the clutches of death over
six times.

Before he knew it, the Benz was pulling up in front of
The Trump Plaza Hotel, the place where money-getters played
at. How exciting this was. Fats and Nut exited the Benz, then
went to the front desk to pay for their rooms. However,
someone they saw, at least they thought, reminded them of the
Bald Man they watched kill Flat-Head in front of them,
forcing them into a deadly beef in which they had barely

survived.

"Who was that, Nut?" Fats asked, looking over his shoulders as the Bald Man headed into the casino.

"I don't know, slim. It jive look like that bamma' that crushed shawdy that morning." Nut responded. They then stepped onto the elevator.

"No bullshit! I was thinking the same damn thing. You got them hammers on you, right?"

"Hell yeah, never leave home without them." Nut smirked, revealing his front chipped tooth smile.

"Good," Fats nodded as the elevator doors closed. The elevator began moving up.

Fats and Nut had there heads down when the elevator reached the tenth floor. The doors opened, revealing the Bald Man. He was pushing a woman in a wheel chair. Fat's and Nut's mouths remained opened, but there were no words to be said. They stared at the Bald Man and the paralyzed woman, both leveling guns with silencers attached to the ends of them.

Just a moan.

Then a muffled scream.

Then incredible pain! The Bald Man and Pepa both opened fire on them, shooting until their magazines emptied.

"Ramel sends his regards and revenge from Flat-Head, Fray, and Brooke." Pepa said softly as the bald killer slammed home a fresh magazine and shot Nut twice in the forehead. He then gave her the gun. Pepa shot Fats in the throat.

The pain exploded into his throat and Fats felt as if he couldn't breathe. He wanted to tell the crying woman in the wheelchair that the man she was with killed Flat and started everything, but he couldn't do that either. Everything was spinning, until down he went, helpless to break his own fall.

Fats might have hit the elevator floor face first, because he didn't even care. Nothing mattered except the incredible death trap he'd just walked into. His vision became fuzzy. The worse pain was of being tricked into death. It was now taking over his body, inhabiting him.

Eastgate Fats heard something. It was the sound of more footsteps approaching the elevator...

Eastgate desperately needed to find out who was there. Who was the mastermind behind the sudden sneak attack? Who was it? Fats couldn't see very well. Everything was so blurry.

"Show yo'self, scared-nigga!" Fats called out, gathering all the strength he could muster. "Don't hide behind no hired guns, you coward-ass-nigga."

Then Fats saw someone walking into the elevator wearing some nile-grey Crocodile lace up shoes. The person wore matching slacks, and a dark-grey turtleneck. Something was familiar about him Fats thought.

"You know revenge is a dish best served cold, Fats. I paid plenty of loot to make this day happen. I even paid off your man, Nut. That's right. And for a quick million he wanted to kill you himself, but I told him to just get you here to me, and I'll handle the rest." Ramel confessed, pulling out a .45 caliber Sig-Sauer. He then screwed on the silencer.

"Wha..." Fats coughed up blood. "Nigga...Fa-fuck you." Fats gasped right before the terrible heat seared his throat and chest. "What you think.... I'ma beg your...coward-ass to spare me? Bitch-nigga, suck... Suck my dic—"

Fats' slick statement got cut off by two Rhino-Head slugs chining into his face, courtesy of Ramel's itchy trigger finger.

After killing Fats he stepped-out of the elevator and glanced at Pepa.

"Ramel, thanks for helping me get some get back for Brooke." Pepa whispered as Ramel walked away without turning back, knowing that he'd die with the truth about who really killed Pepa's lover.

$ $ $

Recognizing the shocking truth that he'd just collected $250,000 because of his reputation as a viscious hitman in D.C.

from one of his previous contract's best friend, who had enough money to set up any person's demise. The Bald Man began pushing Pepa in the direction of the rich record label C.E.O.

The Bald Man walked briskly and noticed that his legs shook a little. For some odd reason, he glanced over his shoulder, then kissed Pepa on top of her head. Maybe it was because he knew that he was saying goodbye to the hitman business.

"What was all that for?" Pepa asked, looking up into the handsome Bald Man's eyes. Ramel had paid the hitman to look after her, at least until they carried out tonight's mission. It had seemed like a good move to hire a fine man to answer her every beck and call, but Pepa had grown emotionally attached to him. Now that the job was done, Pepa didn't know what to expect from him.

Is he really down for me? Or is he after the money that Ramel gives me every month? She asked herself.

"It's for being a down ass chick, for real. Would you mind if I hang around you a little more after today?"

I would love it! Pepa wanted to yell, but she smiled inside and whispered, "If you can put up with me, then I don't mind at all."

"I'm feeling that, and you, Ms. Sexy." The Bald Man smiled as he pushed Pepa towards their reserved hotel suite.

Knowing there was *no turning back* from the new life he wanted to start with someone who needed him, the Bald Man felt it was the least he could do after destroying so many lives in the past.

And there it was, a happy ending for some, if there ever was one. An ex-killer pushing the wheelchair of the first woman he ever truly cared about....

THE END OF THIS STORY
THE BEGINNING OF MANY TO COME
BIG NATION

YOUNG & THUGGIN'

By Troy 'Disco' Jones

Ain't Nobody Pen'in Like Us, Man!!!

Prologue

Beep....Beep....Beep...Beep...Beeeeeeep! The monitor screamed.

"We're losing him!" the nurse said, excitedly.

"Everybody, calm down." The doctor said, rubbing the two fibrillator pads together. "Clear!"

Boop! The electrically charged pads sounded, causing the patient's body to jump.

The doctor rubbed the pads together again. "Clear!"

Boop! The body jumped again.

Beep...Beep...Beep...Beep.

"We've got a pulse!" the nurse yelled. "It's not very strong...if he goes under again, we'll lose him."

"Prep him for surgery...he's lost a lot of blood."

The team of nurses and doctors quickly scrambled to save the young man's life. He'd taken five shots to the back, neck and leg. Shots that were meant to end the life of Troy 'Disco' Jones. Yet, through God and the steady hand of the surgeon, his chances of surviving were increasing by the minute. Either the Grim Reaper had missed his mark or the young certified gangsta was too stubborn to call it quits...

30 DAYS LATER

A month had passed since Disco had been air lifted to Ryder Trauma Center, full of holes and bleeding like a muthafucka. During the course of his stay, he'd caught the attention of Nurse Parrish. Every since she'd laid eyes on him, barely holding on to life, she could not get the handsome young man off of her mind. Everyday after she finished her rounds she would go into his room to check on him, and for the entire time of his stay she never ran into any ladyfriends of his. She found

173

that quite odd, as handsome as he was.

Nurse Parrish was open and aimed to see exactly what it was about Mr. Troy 'Disco' Jones that attracted her so strongly and seemed to repell all others...

Chapter 1

Disco, Lil Will and Maine were sliding down 27th Avenue on their way to Lil Will's babymomma's crib. Normally Disco didn't hang with dudes his age, but with his older brother Pretty Pulla away in Federal prison, he'd hooked up with Lil Will, Maine and their man Jay, and made a few things happen.

"Aye' Sco!" Lil Will called, choking from the lace-blunt he was smoking. "You finna chill wit' us over Trisha crib or what? You know Londa keep askin' about you."

Disco sucked his teeth and cut his eyes at Lil Will, pushing the Chevy Vert like a true big-boy. "Lil Will, you need to keep that mutt-ass-hoe from 'round there, wit' that big, sloppy-ass, nasty pussy...and her head-game ain't on nothin' anyway."

"Man, at least say something to the hoe, 'cause I'm tired of her ass always askin' me 'bout you." Lil Will lightweight begged.

"Will, my nigga, you might as well let Maine hit the hoe, I'm straight. I gotta go pick up Jay and go handle some shit, for real...besides, my nigga, I ain't tryna be 'round no hoe like that. She know my lil' wife and all."

When the '71 Impala convertible pulled up to Will's babymomma's house, a black Chrysler 300 was leaving. Lil Will and Maine jumped out and Disco rolled off 'olo. TRILLA by Rick Ross was beating from the black-on-black convertible as the top slowly came down and the *24"* Ashantis rolled towards Choppa-Locka.

$ $ $

"Trisha, who that was just pulled off in that black 300?"

"I'on know dude. He was here to see Londa." Trisha answered Lil Will with a slight attitude.

"When that pussy-ass-cracka got out the feds?"

Trisha popped her lips. "See boy, you need to touch yo' nose, because White-boy Dave is still in the feds. That was some new dude Londa just met."

"Well why the stupid ass hoe got the nigga comin' round here?" Lil Will stated. "She need to meet buddy somewhere else. You know a nigga got sack in here...you should know better."

No sooner than Lil Will had completed his statement, Londa came out of the front door onto the porch where Trisha, Lil Will and Maine stood talking. She was a bad little chick as far as appearence was concerned. Yet too many dicks in her mouth and pussy had fucked up her reputation.

"Wuz up, Lil Will, Maine?" Londa popped like a true hoodrat. "Ain't that was Disco who just dropped yall off?"

"Yeah, that was fool." Lil Will said. " But Londa, check this out, I need to holla at you right quick."

"'Bout what?"

"'Bout buddy who just left the house. Who was that?"

"Oh, that was my new friend Varray. He from Overtown."

"Why you met the nigga over here? You know this crib off limits." Lil Will barked.

"Nah, Will, he seen all us together on Maine's birthday at the Rollexxx, anyway. It ain't like I just met him. We don' been out a couple times and he asked me to introduce him to Disco. He wanna cop some work or whatever. And I knew that Disco was bringin' yall back."

"Bitch, you don' bumped yo' muthafuckin' head!" Lil Will snapped.

Londa rolled her eyes and sucked her teeth. "First off, Will, I ain't no bitch. I was just tryna plug yall and make me a few dollars. Shit been crazy for me since the feds snatched Dave up."

Stupid ass bitch, Lil Will thought. "Well, yo' ass lucky that nigga pulled off, 'cause Disco woulda fucked you and that nigga up for steppin' to him sideways wit' that bullshit. I gotta lil love for you on the strength of you bein' Trisha's best friend, but you better get yo' fuckin' mind right."

"Well, will you holla at Disco for me, please Will?" Londa begged.

"I'll see what's up." Lil Will said and pulled Trisha in the house.

$$\$ \$ \$$$

Disco pulled up in front of Jay's ole-girl crib in Choppa-Locka. He was beating so hard that he didn't need to blow the horn. Everybody in the eight block vicinity heard his sound system.

Jay came walking out of the house like an old man. "Say bruh, turn that music down. You know that old lady 'cross the street be trippin," he whined, hopping in the vert.

Disco said, "Fuck that lady! You need to move yo' ole-girl from 'round here anyway."

Smashing the gas, the vert snatched off, smoking up the block as Disco cut rubber. He'd just had Alex put a super-charger in his shit and he loved the way it snatched. They balled off of Jay's street and got into the flow of traffic.

"Say bruh," Jay began, talking slow. "You really need to park this shit and jump behind some tints, for real-for real."

Disco ignored him, steady punching the vert. "And you need to stop trippin', we good."

The two *always* went through it. Jay was older than Disco and had been good friends with Disco's older brother, Pretty Pulla. The two met over ten years ago in Largemont Projects, some of the toughest projects in Miami Dade County. Those projects groomed them into the gangstas that they were.

Jay turned down the radio so that Disco could hear him clearly. But Disco didn't even give him a chance to speak. He simply reached over and turned the radio back up, laughing. He loved to fuck with Jay, because even though they were good friends and business partners, Jay somewhat feared

177

Disco. Not that Jay was pussy, he had one or two bodies under his belt, but he simply knew that he could not stand in the paint with Disco. Mainly because Jay or nobody else ever knew Disco's next move.

They were headed to Broward to holla at Disco's little partner, Boe. Disco needed to introduce him to Jay, because he had plans on making Boe part of the family.

"You sho' we can trust buddy? 'Cause I really don't be feelin' these outsider ass niggas, for real-for real." Jay stated.

"I feel you, bruh-bruh, but when I did that lil' bid up at Coleman, all them niggas that was from the crib, always 'round a nigga smokin' a nigga goods and eatin' up a nigga shit, all them hoe-ass niggas left a nigga out there when that shit jumped off wit' me and fool at the poker table...my nigga, them chico's upped swords on me and all. And the only nigga that stood in the paint wit' a nigga was Boe. So yeah, I trust buddy...He gotta mind on him too. While we was locked down behind that fuck-shit, me and him came up wit' a lil' plan. Now it's time to put it down. Feel me?"

$ $ $

Maine and Lil Will were still at Trisha's house cooking up hard and handling the table work. Maine was an animal over the stove. He could easily turn 36 ounces into 54 with his golden wrist and still have tension. For every two ounces that he dropped in the three ounce beaker, he brought back another. And after every 18 ounces he had to change the beaker because they would break under the pressure of his whip game.

After laying down the last three cookies Maine went and sat at the table with Will, the top-table-man in the world. Lil Will could bag up 95 DP's [*$10 bags of cocaine*] off of an ounce, without using cut and still have enough to roll a lace-blunt. That was $34,200 and 36 lace-blunts a brick!

With Maine's wrist, Will's table game, Disco's hustle and Jay's cocaine connect, they were eating real good.

After they were done, Lil Will and Maine jumped in

Trisha's white-on-white SHT Hemi Charger and hit all of their traps, making sure that the workers had plenty of work for their shift.

Pulling out of Silver Blue Lakes, Will made a left on 103rd and then hit 1-95 headed North. When he reached the fish-bowl he caught 826 West, headed to Miami Lakes to drop Maine off.

Even though Disco paid Maine and Lil Will top dollar to lieutenant his spots, they had established their own thing on the side, which was robbing banks. Being from Robin Hood, robbing shit was second nature to them. They'd been snatching pockets, jacking niggas coming out of the Flea Market, and breaking in dope-boys cars and cribs since they were ten and eleven years old. That's how they met Disco in the first place.

Trisha was fucking around with a *green-ass-nigga* from Coconut Grove named Lil Buddy. After Lil Will found out and beat *her* ass, he made Trisha copy the dude's house keys and give them to him and Maine. The two of them then ran off in Lil Buddy's spot and came out of that bitch with 20 pounds of 'Zona, *good green weed,* and 5,000 grams of Olean, *raw cocaine.* Young and ultra-dumb, they sold everything to Disco for $67,000, which they quickly blew on chunk, clothes and two Chevys. Yet they were cool because the deal had made them family.

$ $ $

Maine and Lil Will had been handling banks for a little over a year now. Besides Trisha, nobody knew about their extracurricular activities, and the only reason that she knew was because she was their driver. They'd been together since Westview Junior High and Lil Will trusted her with his life.

"Yo bruh, I been checkin' out this Bank of America in Hialeah and that bitch sweet."

"Yeah? When we gon' slide out there so I can see just how 'sweet' it is?"

"Shid', we can slide through in the morning if you get yo' ass up, yo." Maine said, cutting his eyes at Lil Will. "Cause you been sleepin' like a bitch lately...Let me find out you

179

got Trisha pregnant again, fool."

Lil Will shook his head. "I don't know, dog. I might've fucked up."

Maine bussed up laughing at his dog. "Ain't no pressure, fool... that's just another reason to tear these crackas off and throw another *big-boy* party. You feel me?"

"Yeah, whatever."

The two rode in silence until they reached Maine's crib. He'd had the house for a little over a year. He bought it with his first bank robbery money and he'd spent a very attractive piece of change remodeling it.

"Damn, Maine," Lil Will said, pulling up to the house. "I like what you're doin' to the crib. That bitch tight."

"Bet that up, boy...I'm just tryna keep up wit' that nigga Jay. I don' dropped 'bout $85,000 remakin' that bitch."

"Yeah, well you gon' have to drop 'bout another $85,000 to keep up wit' fool. His shit plushed out!"

"For real," Maine said, getting out of the car. "But yo, fool gettin' all that bread and livin' in a *big-boy* crib like that...my nigga, why he got his ole-girl still squattin' in the hood like that?"

"I don't know, but that's something that Jay gotta worry 'bout. I'm worryin' 'bout Bank of America in Hialeah."

"I heard that," Maine shot back.

The two exchanged dap and Maine walked off towards his front door.

His crib really was nice. He smiled to himself, admiring his work and feeling good about how far he'd came. Maine never noticed the dude dressed in all black squatting beside the hedges. Without warning the man spung from the bushes pointing an AK-47.

"Yeah, buddy! You know what time it is!"

No sooner than those words left his mouth two more dudes with guns ran from the side of the house. They made Maine open the door and disarm the alarm system. *Damn!* Maine cursed himself. The three men were wearing ski masks, so Maine figured that they hadn't came to kill.

"We came for the money and the work, playa. Simple

robbery, buddy. Don't make it a homicide, nigga!"

The dude with the rusty looking Choppa was doing all of the rapping.

Maine was a seasoned jack-boy before he ever knew anything about drugs, so he knew two things: one was that they didn't want to splash him or they wouldn't have wore masks; and two, he could see that they weren't real robbers, because they were to jumpy and they were talking too damn much. That alone made him want to buck bad-as-hell! But like Boo Baby said, *when you know better, you do better.* So Maine laid it down and followed their instructions.

They led him to the car garage and handcuffed him to the crash bar of his Range Rover. There was thirty-something thousand in the headboard of his King size bed, his Cuban-link chain and bracelet, plus his 14kt gold Jaeger LeCouitre watch were all in his dresser draw, and he did not waste anytime telling them where it was all at. He even told them about the case of Armand De Cognac [Ace of Spade] that he had in his storage closet. Maine wanted to let them know about the 14 grams of clean and the five dime bags of weed that he'd just got out of Silver Blue Lake Apartments, but he knew that when they left he *was* going to need something to smoke, to calm his nerves.

Now what he didn't tell them was about the big hidden wall safe in the guest room closet with the $240,000 re-up money and Disco's Audemars Piquet watch in it. He also didn't tell them that they were all dead niggas once he figured out exactly what the lick read and who put them on it.

The three masked robbers took what they could and slid off. But not before Maine peeped the tattoo on the wrist of the dude with the AK-47. It read T4L [*Tower For Life*].

$ $ $

As Lil Will whipped off from Maine's crib, he came to a four-way stop sign and noticed that the police were camped out up ahead of him with their lights off. *Fuck!* Lil Will said to himself and yoked it hard to avoid a problem with the crackas. That's when he

181

noticed Maine's cellphone slide off of the seat and onto the floor. He didn't even pick it up, he just bussed a U-turn and flushed it back to Maine's crib to give him his phone....

ONE LOVE

PLEX

BOOK GANG MEDIA
PO Box 2114
Clinton, MD 20735
(301) 856-7797

Shipping address

Name:_____

Address:_____

City:_____State:_____Zip:_____

Title	Author	Price
STREET RAISED: The Beginning	Mike Harper	15.95
BOO BABY: The Secret Of...	PLEX	15.95
SERVED: With No Regard!	PLEX	15.95
STREET RAISED: The Raw Deal	PLEX	15.95
NO TURNING...	Big Nation	13.95
PROMISCUOUS	Calvin Williams	14.95
CRUMBS TO BRICKS	Capo Cat	15.95
SUGAR	Mike Harper	15.95
PRISON STORIES	Seth Ferranti	15.00
STREET LEGENDS Vol. 1	Seth Ferranti	15.00
STREET LEGENDS Vol. 2	Seth Ferranti	15.00
ONE LOVE	PLEX	13.95
BUCKIN 'DA 'DICE	Book Gang	15.95
LIL ONE: Blood Investment	K-1 & Bino	15.00
LOVE & THUGGIN'	Bo Brown	15.95
GET IT HOW YOU LIVE	Big Gemo	13.95
EROTIC DESIRES	Seven Supreme	13.95

3.75(S&H) for 1-3 Books _____
For Quantities over 3 add $ .75 per book _____

188

www.ingramcontent.com/pod-product-compliance
Lightning Source LLC
Chambersburg PA
CBHW060937180626
46817CB00004B/1598